FAMILY!

Books by Fannie Hurst

NONFICTION
Anatomy of Me (An Autobiography)

NOVELS
Family!
The Man with One Head
Newspaper
The Hands of Veronica
Hallelujah
Lonely Parade
Great Laughter
Anitra's Dance
Imitation of Life
Back Street
Five and Ten
A President Is Born
Appassionata
Lummox
Star-Dust

SHORT STORIES
We Are Ten
Procession
Song of Life
The Vertical City
Humoresque
Gaslight Sonatas
They Stood Like Stone
Just Around the Corner

MISCELLANY
No Food with My Meals
Today Is Ladies' Day
Land of the Free
If I to Laugh
Anonymous

FAMILY!

A NOVEL

Fannie Hurst

Doubleday & Company, Inc.
Garden City, New York

ALL OF THE CHARACTERS IN THIS BOOK
ARE FICTITIOUS, AND ANY RESEMBLANCE
TO ACTUAL PERSONS, LIVING OR DEAD,
IS PURELY COINCIDENTAL.

FAMILY!

Chapter 1

MAN IN A SMALL HOUSE
ON A SMALL STREET

A MAN IN A SMALL HOUSE ON A SMALL STREET IN A SUBURB of St. Louis was suddenly finding himself gripped by a compulsion to look inward.

Not given to this kind of scrutiny, it irked. It was not so much that he liked not what he saw. On the contrary, it was tidy in there. But that very tidiness bothered him. How unremarkable could a man be?

What induced this inward stare might have happened to almost any average citizen across the nation, living in a small house on a small street.

But the incident, a trivial one, happened to happen to Ed Sprague.

Except for the biological circumstance of two zygotes' splitting and making twins, Ed and Clara Sprague might have enjoyed a twenty-five-day flight around the world, an Imperial Deep Freeze, a Masterpiece Hi-Fi, and a year's supply of Delovely Frozen Food Products.

9

But instead, a family named Karelson in Great Falls, Montana, was chosen "Average American Family" by the *National Homemaker Magazine*, chiefly because twins made the Sprague family a mite special, whereas the Karelsons' two children were a conventional eighteen months apart.

Clara had been as bitter over this hairline miss as it was in her nature to be about anything. "Don't tell me 'A miss is as good as a mile'! I wouldn't have minded it half as much if we hadn't lost out on just that one count."

"On that *two* count, you mean, Mom. Twins."

"I don't care so much for myself, Anchutz, but your father has had so little out of it except nose-to-the-grindstone. At least I've seen Niagara Falls."

Actually, except for this brief travel interlude before her marriage, neither had Clara's olfactory feature been spared the grindstone.

Ed had reiterated as much the Sunday morning they sat on the front porch, the *Homemaker Magazine* open between them as they flipped page after page of photographs of the Karelson "Average American Family."

The Karelsons in their living room around the television set. The Karelsons descending their veranda steps on their way to Sunday-morning church services. The Karelsons on a picnic; gardening; preparing a cookout; inspecting a litter of puppies; absorbed in a do-it-yourself paint job on the garage.

"When you come right down to it," ruminated Ed, pulling at his pipe, "neither the Karelsons nor us have lived it up the high-wide-and-handsome way. Average American Family, backbone of the nation, whatever that means. Whatever we are, it suits me."

"Me too, Ed. 'Togetherness' don't get a laugh out of me. It suits me just fine."

Clara, who had allowed her breasts to sag, and her hair to gray, had never worn an uplift or cut her hair. Without concession to changing fashions, she continued to arrange her gray hair in a twist slightly to the rear of the top of her head, four bone hairpins of matching gray holding the bun in place.

Originally there had been six of these, but, with two lost or broken, she had managed with four. Once, during the series of interviews with the representative of *Homemaker Magazine*, one of the four had dropped to the floor, her interrogator handing it back to her.

"Dear me, I wouldn't want to lose that. I've worn these same hairpins for about eighteen years," laughed Clara.

Her interviewer had been intrigued by this small circumstance. "You are obviously a thrifty wife, Mrs. Sprague."

"Oh, this wasn't exactly thrift. One gets used to doing things the same way. But I must say, one needs to be thrifty in our walk of life."

Clara's way of smiling was a deepening of the fan-shaped spray of wrinkles at the corners of her eyes.

"Guess the same pretty well applies to you, Mr. Sprague?"

Ed, who was balding and paunching, hiked up his crossed leg by the ankle. "It's been up to all of us to be that way, young fellow. Been a salaried man all my life."

"Do I understand, sir, thirty-six years with one firm?"

"Thirty-seven, come June. Started with the Henschen Brothers Mercantile Company as a stock boy."

"Henschen Brothers Mercantile? That name is known in the East."

"Largest firm of the kind in the Midwest."

"My husband could have been a high-up by now if he had driven himself," commented Clara placidly and without rancor. "We don't believe in high tension. Now, take my husband's brother Charley. He had the temperament for driving himself to the top."

"The wife is right there," agreed Ed Sprague with equal placidity. "My brother Charley, and John Henry too, for that matter, rate I guess with the twenty or twenty-five richest men in St. Louis, and they grew up no different than I did, right here in West Grove."

"Were you a West Grove girl, Mrs. Sprague?"

"No, I was born on Gratiot Street in South St. Louis. My husband and I never met until we were grown. But you might say we come from the same town, West Grove being a suburb of the big town."

"And you never saw fit to join your brothers in their enterprises, Mr. Sprague?"

"My brother Charley made his first big money on an electrical propeller device he bought from the fellow who invented it and who worked in the electrical supply shop where Charley did. Maybe you've heard of it. The Peerless Self-Propeller."

"Not exactly in my line, Mr. Sprague."

"Don't have to be to have heard of it. Well, anyway, Charley at that time was already beginning to show his knack for turning almost anything he touched into gold by making little deals outside his job. Well, he comes to John Henry and me to buy in on the propeller."

"John Henry did what Ed didn't do," interposed Clara, again with complete placidity, "and bought in."

"Yep, my brothers made their first fortune on that deal—royalties still coming in."

"I always say if Charley hadn't started his fortune on that deal it would have been on the next."

"Too bad for you."

"Ed and I don't feel like that. John Henry was not married at the time, but our children were babies, and we had saved up exactly the amount of the investment, all the security we had, against sickness."

"Besides," added Ed, "we didn't——" and stopped short.

"Go on, say it, Ed." When the silence continued, Clara moved into it. "It's nothing against his brothers, Mr. Reporter. It was an out-and-out business transaction; the inventor sold it of his own free will for more money than he had ever seen in his life—which was precious little, it is true. But who knows, except for Charley, he might not have sold it at all. Anyway, that is one way of looking at it," concluded Clara, a little lamely.

"Sure thing. Charley was within his rights."

"But Ed and I got to talking it over, just for the sake of argument and never really thinking it would happen, that if the propeller should happen to make a fortune, it would leave the fellow who invented it nowhere."

"No reflection on my brothers!"

"Certainly not. It was just that my husband and I weren't big-money ambitious, because even after that, Charley offered us a few investment chances which we didn't accept. I guess we just naturally think little and they think big."

"Have you ever regretted it?"

"Never a day, except sometimes maybe for the children's

sake, not that they were denied as much education as they wanted."

"Nope," agreed Ed, pulling away at his pipe. "Never regretted it."

14

Chapter 2

UNEVENTFUL FACES

BOTH CLARABELLE AND HER BROTHER ANCHUTZ HAD the uneventful faces that fade quickly in the memory. People would remark, particularly of Anchutz: "I recall having met him, but I can't remember what he looks like."

In contrast, the bright beauty of Charley's children stood out in a kind of sunlight. Clara often observed, but with lack of envy: If Clarabelle only had the opportunities to be brought out of herself! After all, typing in a law office could not do for a girl's looks what beauty parlors and facials can.

Continued Clara to herself: It's not the overly handsome but the passably nice-looking men who are the dependables. In addition to Anchutz's quiet nature, working in the same firm with his father, eating his lunch with him most of the time, hammering and sawing away with him down in the basement workroom instead of stepping out with the girls, don't get a young man out of himself.

One evening Clarabelle, on her way to a supper and

bazaar in the basement of the church, came downstairs in a new blue taffeta dress and matching hat.

Her parents, standing side by side, contemplated her.

"Clarabelle," exclaimed Clara, "I'm glad you bought the blue instead of the brown!"

"You look mighty pretty, daughter."

"Oh, Papa, you know *pretty* isn't the word for me."

"Well, pretty is as pretty does."

"Please, Papa," cried Clarabelle, "it's terrible to always be told—that!" Recovering herself, she kissed him. "It's enough just to seem pretty to you and Mama," she added, through a hard core of hurting.

Even so, despite incidents such as this, Clara, as she viewed her children's cousins across the width of West Grove, preferred it the way it was. However financially well placed, Charley's two were in a zone of dangerous living. Neither of her chicks ventured far from the nest or wanted to, and even with the inherent heartaches, she rejoiced.

She wished of course that Ed's long years of loyal service had rewarded him better and that his ultimate retirement would yield more than the slender pension and gold watch from the firm. She wished that Anchutz, by circumstance and preference, did not seem destined to follow in his father's plodding footsteps. He too would one day deserve better of the years. She wished that Clarabelle wore outwardly more of her inward beauty and that the years of her fleeting girl-hood were doing more to assuage her hungering spirit. All this she wished, but through an unmarred serenity. Yes, regarding Ed's better-placed brothers, their wives, their children, Clara still wanted it the way it was.

To be sure, she would have coveted for either or both of

them the talent of John Henry's wife, Myra Goldonsky, who was musically known locally and played piano recitals before ladies' clubs throughout the state. Yet what kind of a life did Myra and John Henry enjoy? A wife of career but no children, the elegant little home womanless during Myra's recital tours.

It was fifteen years since Charley's wife, Polly, was discovered sitting beside the great Gothic fireplace in their living room, sticking pins as far as she could force them into her wrist.

This precipitated what had been an encroaching condition over a protracted period, and Polly became a permanent resident at Dr. Schwimmer's "nursing home" up near Chain of Rocks.

Notwithstanding the separateness which had established itself between the Ed Spragues and the brothers, Clara, however remote her way of life, would have stepped in at this stage with all possible aid to Charley's disorganized family. But Brock and Claudia, already largely on their own, were still in preparatory schools, and it was common knowledge that Charley, while his wife had been slipping out of his world into hers of hallucinations, had found compensations in his work.

Many were tolerant. What could you expect? Years of no wife. The poor dear should have been put away long ago. Charley had done his part—the best doctors, nurses, the children sent off to the best schools. A man of his wealth was still young enough to want a life for himself. But according to rumor, what a life. A man who could pick selectively, choosing associations in the downtown areas of St. Louis . . .

It must all have been too much for poor Polly Deitz,

who, when she married Charley, had been the pretty only daughter of a one-time streetcar conductor who had later amassed a considerable fortune in building contracting.

Who could have foreseen, although it later developed that there had been mental instability on her mother's side, that Polly Deitz would end in permanent mental collapse?

And just look at the children, Clara would reason to herself. What had they to show for all their advantages? If you measured them against her two . . .

Inheriting, upon reaching the age of twenty-one, about one hundred thousand dollars each from their late maternal grandfather had only served to introduce new hazards into their pampered lives.

Not but what Clara could truthfully say she could have wished her own father had been in a position to do as much or one tenth as much for Clarabelle and Anchutz. Dear knows, they would have reacted differently.

But just look at Brock! Married to a doll-faced tramp at twenty-four. Divorced from her at twenty-five. In the newspapers for a record number of speeding offenses. And last, but dreadfully not least, suspected of being one of those solitary drinkers who allegedly disappear periodically for a week or even weeks at a time. As Clara understood it, Brock's absences from his office in one of his father's real estate projects were increasingly frequent. You never would have suspected it. Brock at thirty still had that blond Greek-runner look, his eyes as electric-blue as his mother's had been.

Take his sister, Claudia, married to as nice a fellow as Clara estimated you could find in a thousand. A professional baseball player, it is true, but when Claudia married him not only a big earner but an idol locally and nationally. What had she done with her life? Tossed it over. And for what? sniffed Clara. For want of appreciation of what a fine fellow she had, who when he retired from baseball wanted to support her on his own. Mind you, a girl that wasn't willing to keep up her husband's self-respect and live on his earnings instead of on her money, thus reducing him to one of those gigolos! Could you imagine her Clarabelle doing a thing like that? Why, Clarabelle would have given up the pretty house Claudia and Frank had lived in during his professional baseball years and settled down with him in one room if need be. Clara had even heard, from a certain neighbor—and somehow she had not confided this to any member of her family—that since her divorce Claudia was "sleeping around."

Clara could weave away at such thoughts as if knitting needles were flashing inside her head. No siree. She wouldn't want the lives of the Charley or John Henry families if you gave them to her. Crack-ups, divorces, overindulged children lacking a mother's guidance. The fine house full of homelessness. John Henry's home empty half the time, while the wife ran around the state, piano-playing.

If that was life, they could have it.

Yet sitting on the porch beside Ed that Sunday morning, the magazine containing the photographic spread of the winning "Average American Family" open between them, pangs of regret that they had missed being it by a hairline would not quite squash down. If they had won that trip around the world, who knows what it might have done for the jog-trot of her children's lives? Not that they would have tolerated that description, but her shipping-clerk son and stenographer daughter deserved better.

Anchutz and Clarabelle needed to be brought out of themselves. They had had so little.

Chapter 3

ONE HELL OF A WOMAN

A MAN SAT WITH HIS HEAD IN HIS HANDS. ATTITUDE: dejection. A large ornate drawing room, pale as a ghost, cool and underemphasized by a professional decorator's hand, seemed to stand off from him. He was a big, overweight man who would have been perspiring except that his house was air conditioned from basement-billiard room to the top-floor suite with the window bars, that Polly had occupied before her move to the nursing home.

Up there, fat, uncorseted, her face a wasteland, she had sat counting her fingers, banging away at the windowpane, or singing into the long hours in a voice which, once a clear little soprano trained in her church choir, had taken on the hard crackle of a parrot.

When Charley, as was his wont, went up daily to visit her, she either shrilled at him abusively or went back to her bridehood, when she had been lovely, and attempted to lay herself into his arms, which filled him with horror.

21

People said of him that, with all his wealth, his life had been bogged down with tragedy, not only by the long-time disturbed wife but by children who presented him with problems.

But Charley, with his head in his hands, was thinking of women. More specifically, of a woman, and in terms of self-justification. A man, he was reasoning, if he is realistic, must face up to the fact that at sixty-four he is entering the November years of his life. He felt entitled to "live them up." A man would be crazy not to.

After all, for some years he had been legally entitled to divorce poor Polly. But something in him forbade such a step. Paradoxically, he felt he owed little to either Brock or Claudia. Both were long since out of the nest, and although now they were both free to return to it, neither had offered to make that move. Not that he blamed them. The years away at schools and the traveling vacations had rooted them nowhere.

What he did owe them, if anything, was respect for their dead mother, and to the Sprague name in general, and of course to the family standing in the church where he enjoyed official capacity.

His own tiny ninety-pound widowed mother who had dominated her three sons all the way into their manhood, educating them halfway through high school on earnings from a notion store, had also educated them to Methodism, conforming behavior and attitudes.

The three men-sons beside her bier, as it was lowered into its yawn of earth, had stood there bareheaded, a great deal of her remaining back in each of them.

Charley needed the security of feeling himself a standout

in the community. Thanks largely to that pint-size mother, who between minding a fatherless household and dispensing pins, dress shields and sleeve garters, had found time to direct the religious education of her boys, his church affiliations as a member of the board and usher buttressed those needs.

Sunday mornings, in striped trousers and frock coat, with John Henry and Ed in similar attendance, Charley had a sense of the Sprague status as he escorted solid citizens down the aisle.

This sense of security had been shaken the morning, eighteen years before, when John Henry had come to him with the intention, subject always to his older brother's reaction, of marrying a young lady, a Miss Myra Goldonsky, whom he had met in a railroad station through a mutual acquaintance.

"Goldonsky? A Jewish young lady and in addition, you say, two years older than you? With all the world to choose from, why in heaven's name need it be a Jewish girl?"

"Because, Charley, I like her. I suppose I more than like her, I—guess I love her. You see for yourself how long it has taken me to meet such a one."

That was true enough. John Henry was well into his thirties.

As a matter of fact, Charley had never given thought to the problem of minorities. Prejudices had only had occasion to stir languidly, if at all. Most Jews were supposed to be shrewd, but this one made her living by playing the piano and teaching. It had taken a Jewish girl to capture a rich bachelor over and above the local girls. Not that Charley had anything against Jews, but in the family was another matter.

23

There had been a Ben Grossman who had worked beside Charley in the War Supplies Department with whom he had enjoyed compatibility and who, up to the present, never failed to call on him when passing through St. Louis.

Grossman was a rich man. Most Jews were, it seemed, from the names associated with St. Louis big business. Bernheimer Brothers. Lazarus and Mintz. Lederman, Inc. Rauh and Sons.

From his own experience they were not as shrewd as they were purported to be. On the contrary, next to the propeller, he had made one of his most advantageous deals with the inventor, named Isaacs, of a truck-loading device, now in international use.

He did not recall any people of "the Hebraic faith," as he expressed it, in his childhood, with the exception of the old-clothes men who came periodically to the front door, and Moishe the Tailor and Presser at the corner whose son Sholem was taunted by neighborhood youngsters because he was not permitted to join them on Saturdays in the vacant lot for baseball or marbles.

But in the end, John Henry's ultimate marriage to Myra Goldonsky caused no appreciable ripple. Rather strangely, it was a matter of little comment, except among mothers who had placed their chicks in his path during his bachelorhood.

That contemplation brought Virgie around to the front of Charley's revolving mind. Dared he! Episode John Henry was now a matter of eighteen years back. But despite the fact that John Henry was to remain little more than the tail to Charley's kite, and despite Ed's consistent separateness,

Charley had meanwhile become importantly cemented into
the community.

Therefore, dared he?

During the long, long years of Polly's incarceration his
aloneness had forced him in the direction of women who had
intimated, if not suggested, that he divorce Polly. One, the
St. Louis widow of a former business associate to whom he
had thereafter given short shrift, had even urged it.

That was the beauty of Virgie. In the months since he
had been basking in the warmth of her he could have sworn
that such a thought had never entered her yellowed head.
Virgie lived by the hour, asking nothing of the one behind
or the one ahead.

He was thinking of her with his head in his hands. She
was one hell of a woman. She was five women in one, big
nature, big bosom, big heart and big fun. And stories!
Virgie could spin a yarn that from any other woman would
be—well, never mind. But when it came from Virgie, just
big-natured big fun.

If ever a woman deserved better than the life she lived!
But for the life of him, Charley could not be quite sure what
kind it was. Sufficient unto the day, he had a habit of telling
himself, as he dropped in on her with growing frequency.

But suddenly and without warning, this was not enough.
It had begun to irk. He wanted her for himself. She was one
hell of a woman. He could afford ten times over to have her
for himself. But the woman had no wants. In a way Polly,
in the good years, had been like that, keeping the good jewels
he gave her in a safe-deposit box and wearing only her plain
wide wedding band.

Virgie kept his sole gift, a small brooch of tiny emeralds

25

and diamonds, lying loose in a drawer in the four-room flat she occupied over a corner grocery store in an old section of St. Louis, where the one-time good residences had become rooming houses or two-family dwellings.

Charley justified to himself this bracketing of Polly and Virgie in his thoughts. A man could do no more for the memory of a wife than by choosing in her successor some of her same virtues.

The town might not recognize Virgie, blond and flamboyant, for what she was, but he knew her for what she was. A hell of a woman, sure to be good both in and out of bed.

His growing relationship with her was nobody's business. Certainly not poor Polly's, who had been worse than dead long before her death. Neither was it the affair of his self-centered children, who were grown, financially on their own, and no longer in residence with him.

John Henry knew about Virgie, and although Charley had told it in great confidence, it was fair to assume that by now Myra also knew.

Failure to count Ed in on a matter of such close family interest was not because he had got himself nowhere. But the Ed Spragues had long since practically taken themselves outside the family periphery, their paths seldom crossing.

Charley, who was a stickler for credit where credit was due, could testify that he had done his part. His conscience was clear. Had he not, in that now historic propeller deal, which had started their fortune, extended Ed the same opportunity he had to John Henry? Of the two at that time, Ed probably had more put by than John Henry.

Charley was not one to be refused, although in Ed's case he did follow up with an invitation to him to come in on a second deal. Chilean copper this time, and again Ed had declined.

This rigidity of purpose stemmed from Ed's boyhood. He had always been as independent as a hog on ice. Look where it had got him! Life on a treadmill, his wife and two children there with him. A small man thinks small. That was Ed. Live small. Die small.

Polly used to say it had all been the fault of Clara, who was so afraid of being "beholden." Well, she had her way, and the Ed Spragues were living it out in the rambling wooden house, gray for want of paint, over on Bertie Street. No siree, no more overtures after that!

Not that he would ever let Ed want. But how Charley lived his life was none of Ed's affair, because he had chosen it that way. Virgie was damn well none of Ed's business! The great big bag of blowy blondness, God bless her, was Charley's own business. He felt warmed at the very sight of her, and for a man who through the years had been chilled to the bone, beat that if you can.

He could see her now, through his tightly closed lids, in that violently furnished little front room of her apartment over the grocery store, which you entered by way of an outside staircase up the flank of the building. A huge Japanese paper fan, a gift from her son his first year in service, covered the space over the mantelpiece; strewn dolls and fancy pillows were everywhere. The portieres into the bedroom made soft clatter as you walked through them into an equally gimcracky bedroom, and Virgie warming it all up. One hell of a woman.

Chapter 4

HE SAT ALONE

IT WAS COMING HOME TO CHARLEY MORE AND MORE, particularly in moments of head-in-hands contemplation, that perhaps he should not have retired from or disposed of so many of his enterprises. His mind, his body were still too active.

The years of his immersion in large promotional ventures, packed with speculative real-estate transactions, building and mining ventures, had been so short, the days so quick, the evenings, when Polly was in robust bloom, filled with what seemed in retrospect a kind of pleasant fatigue when it was good to be home, slippered feet up, and Polly upstairs bathing the young children, their splashings and her admonishings filling the house with the sounds of a home.

During World War Two, Charley's participation in the Washington War Supplies Department had been his sole respite, thirteen months of it, from the pressures of speculative promotion, his luck running precariously, and consistently, high.

Now he had stepped aside, as he contended a statesman, a prizefighter, or his star baseball player son-in-law should, before one's career began its almost inevitable down-trek from the mountaintop.

After months of negotiations, intricacies, legalities, gone were the major concerns with which he had lived and lain awake nights during the high-tension years of wars, postwars, cold wars, and the manifold problems that went with the Franklin Roosevelt, the Truman, the Eisenhower administrations as they affected the economic climate, tariffs, taxes, stocks and industry.

Following these withdrawals and almost complete retirement from his major projects, Charley no longer subscribed to the *Wall Street Journal* or waited in his dressing gown at the front door each early morning for the paper boy to hurl the twist of St. Louis *Globe-Democrat* onto the veranda.

His mental insulation, even against the big freeze of the cold war with Russia, the red dawn of the atomic era and the threats to world security and his own, was airtight.

Charley had receded snugly into what compensations he could find within each passing hour. Sufficient unto the day. Virgie!

To be sure, there were still winding-up processes hanging fire in the wake of such conclusive transactions as the sale to a corporation of the immense Sprague warehouses on the St. Louis waterfront, a matter of millions; the disposing of several holding companies; selling his controlling shares in the Polly Silver Mines—one of his few major losses, but with tax advantages. And last, maneuvering himself from the presidency of the Interstate Trucking Company to chairman of the board. Affairs of such proportion did not snap off as suddenly as a twig.

The few real-estate projects—a housing development in the suburb of Kirkwood, the management of a block of one-story stores in West Grove, and a couple of small properties near Chain of Rocks, St. Louis—he had retained largely as busywork for his son. Brock had tried in his way, but had never caught on in any of these enterprises in which his father had tried to interest him, including a position he had obtained for him as manager of a supermarket in Belleville, Illinois.

A war, to be sure, had interceded and snatched Brock off for six months in Korea, where he had never been under fire; but, ironically, no sooner had he returned home than he smashed up in an automobile accident, which resulted in concussion and a broken arm. It had to be faced that with apparently good enough intentions, Brock was chiefly ac-complished at being a rich man's son, also wealthy in his own right, but a conservative spender. His sister Claudia laughingly labeled him "tightwad," which he was not. The young and acquisitive wife whom he divorced the second year of their marriage had retired with plentiful jewels and more than generous alimony. Charley often found himself wondering what Polly might have made of Brock or, for that matter, of both their children. Why and how had he, their father, failed them along their way?

For a time he had suspected Brock of secret drinking or worse, but the actual evidence was not there. The boy just didn't have what it takes, or if he did, he had not yet found it. There had been terrible angers between Brock and his father, to the point where Claudia, one zero-weather day, had run out of the house, bareheaded and coatless. But the years had banked the fires of Charley's tempers until they seemed almost to have flickered out.

Charley had aged, they said of him. Retirement is bad for an active man.

Undoubtedly he sat alone in the midst of his new leisure. Yet what, he asked himself, could he expect? Year after year his children away at school. Filling in their summers with friends acquired at these schools had seemed all right at the time. Then came their incredibly sudden adulthood, followed by quick marriages, further removing them. What could you expect? How vacant must be their memories of home life.

Was this sitting alone, Charley wondered, retribution? Was the problem of Brock, nearing thirty and still floundering, part of it? And Claudia, so pretty, so aimless, her first marriage needlessly broken in two as you would a match. And for what? The things that could be bought. . . .

Bah, what the hell! He should not have retired if he could use his leisure only to allow thoughts of this kind to crowd into it. An active man rode life with his spurs in its flanks. Was he now going to allow life to ride him! He didn't intend to! Not by a long shot.

Chapter 5

RISK THE RISKS

COULD IT BE, CHARLEY CONTINUED TO RUMINATE BE-
hind his hands, that of the three brothers, Ed, whose life had
stood still in the shipping department of Henschen Brothers,
had not been the dumb dolt after all?

Nonsense. Charley supposed if he had it to do over he
would do the same thing. Play for high stakes, win, and
know when to retire. After all, how long dare a man in his
sixties, with scarcely a break in his luck, risk the risks?

In her well days, when Polly had been plump and ready
with laughter, Charley had secretly chalked up his successes
to his golden gift of intuition. He was a great one to "feel
things in his bones." Ever since the first hot flash that had
prompted him to buy the propeller, he had played his flashes
for all they were worth, which proved to be millions. Those
Sprague warehouses on acreage that had increased eighty per
cent in value at the time he sold. The food-packing corporation about which he knew little except that the profits rolled.

The four or five patents following the propeller, which he had either bought outright or promoted.

St. Louis promoters said of him: "Everything Charley Sprague touches turns to platinum."

"You mean uranium," John Henry had once corrected.

A surge of greed to live his remaining years to their fullest in directions other than the financial kill rushed over him as he sat there. He wanted that woman down on Pine Street. Virgie had high spirits before which Polly's paled. Zest for life. That's what he had too, plenty of it left in him. Zest for Virgie. Her ebullience pulled him upward with her, as if she were a balloon in ascent.

Virgie had wit with a generous dash of vulgarity, natural vulgarity, paprika to a man whose palate had been so long unexcited. Virgie, in a mood for it, could tell a story to make your hair stand up, except that Charley was balding. Vulgarities were as natural to her as her strong white teeth or her slightly oversized bosom. Overripe as a fine big peach that gave slightly to the touch, was his way of thinking of her. She was what she was. Charley, tethered for so long, had reached a stage where he could not get her out of his consciousness. A hell of a woman.

Chapter 6

IF ONLY

ORIGINALLY MYRA GOLDONSKY SPRAGUE HAD WANTED A ranch house, chiefly for its picture windows. She fancied the great plate-glass sheets, designed to bring the outdoors indoors.

But the split-level layout was impractical because of lack of privacy for Myra, who spent part of each day at her piano. John Henry concurred.

They had just about decided to postpone a move, remain in their suite in the Chase Hotel in St. Louis, which overlooked Forest Park and the distant towers of Washington University and which they had occupied for almost a decade, when Brock alerted them to a ten-year-old, well-built Georgian house in West Grove that was about to be put up for sale.

A ten-minute walk from the Charley Spragues, in the center of about three city lots of well-groomed lawn, the purchase price only slightly beyond the sum they had set

34

as their limit, Myra's decision was born at first glance. She had tried to enlist John Henry's participation in this matter of their first home, but he had disclaimed any part of it.

"She has more judgment about such matters in her little finger than I have in my entire body," was his usual rejoinder when called upon to take part in a decision.

This attitude would doubtless have held true in his business dealings, except that he was seldom called upon to make decisions. Charley saw to them.

Since that first critical decision in the early years, when he had decided to cast his savings into Charley's propeller project, John Henry had followed the pattern of his childhood, depending upon the initiative of his older brother. "The Lord put the brains for us three brothers in one head, Charley's," John Henry conceded cheerfully. "Look where Ed has got without him. Nowhere fast, and nobody to blame but himself."

Over the years John Henry had racked his brains to understand Ed. "Damned if I can make him out. He'll live and die like one of the Anheuser Busch Brewery contented dray horses, three meals a day only not so well fed, the roof to that ramshackle frame house of his over on Bertie Street over his head, two raises and a wrist watch to show for his thirty-fifth year with Henschen Brothers, a wife and children whose faces, for the life of me, I can't remember the minute they're out of my sight."

Myra was not so sure regarding Ed. There was something about the fellow, his independence of his well-placed brothers, his adherence to his way of life—there was just something about it. . . .

Not that Myra would have countenanced his philosophy

of life. Business was business, and Charley had bought the propeller for an out-and-out sum in an out-and-out deal. Not even the Reverend Polkinhorne would have endorsed Ed's passivity. Ed was mealy-minded. And it occurred to Myra, laughingly, that Ed's children were mealy-looking. As in the case of their parents, one was never quite comfortable around them. One felt that like their father, they were regarding John Henry and Charley through the intervening shadowy features of Levi Prothero, inventor of the propeller, who had died in a nursing home sustained by the city.

Well, even if such unfortunate circumstance was the case, Ed and John Henry had certainly not known about it until after his death. Besides, no one had held a gun to Levi Prothero's head and said, "Sell your propeller to me." As a matter of fact, Prothero, needing the ready money, had pursued Charley with it. Oh no, you could never convince Myra Goldonsky that there was not something deeper than Charley's business methods motivating Ed's unwillingness to have any part of his older brother's business dealings. Jealousy, in all probability.

Not that Myra herself entertained illusions about what she secretly termed the "Sprague outfit." Poor Polly, even in her good years, had been a fuddy-duddy, both Brock and Claudia undisciplined and alien to their parents from childhood.

But of her husband, Myra had grown fonder through the years. To be sure, he was not what you could call high powered. But generous to a fault, he was undemanding, easy to live with, and from the time of their marriage, rich! She had reckoned with all this. What had a girl, breadwinner for herself and widowed mother, who had never before had an offer of marriage, to lose?

All her life Myra had chafed and, under the orthodoxy of her Russian-born parents, experienced embarrassment in bringing schoolmates into their small home. During his lifetime her father, carrying his kosher lunch in a brown paper bag, had done long service in the alterations department of Levenson Brothers, a merchant tailoring establishment.

At his death his small life insurance had set her mother up in a pint-size candy and stationery store opposite a schoolhouse. The penny enterprise had carried Myra through high school and a sound pianistic training.

Despite the immemorial wail of anguish that went up from the mother at her only child's marrying into an alien faith, Myra had gone through the ceremony with John Henry in the office of a justice of the peace with few misgivings. Indeed the Sprague family experienced far more. Was John Henry out of his mind, considering the choices he might have made? A Jewish girl, a poor one at that, from nowhere, and on top of it, not even looks! Myra knew she was swarthy, and the nose not good. Musical talent was fine, but John Henry had not a musical note in his body.

Sometimes Myra seemed to regard her husband, with whom she enjoyed compatibility, as if she had never seen him before. Who are you? What do I miss in you? I am what I am, and you are what you are. I do not think about the differences between us. I only feel them. What are you?

John Henry, had he known, would have refuted all this as woman-nonsense. And yet almost periodically there had been telling slips. The day he caught himself too late: "That damn Jew is out to become mayor and run this town." Or: "It beats the Jews the way that fellow can screw you down on prices." On one occasion it had gone far deeper. "See that man over there at the table near the window?" John Henry had remarked one evening in a restaurant. "No, no, not that one. The one next to the woman with the Jew nose."

Myra had felt herself turn into flame. It was not misshapen, only large, somewhat like her own. And somehow "Jewish nose" would not have brought on the same shock occasioned by "Jew nose."

John Henry had the grace to say nothing further, but Myra sensed that he was stung by the mishap of the tongue. He was really a nice fellow, and after a while beneath the table his hand stole over to hers.

That caress was all that was ever spoken between them, but the incident, along with others of similar innocence, lay across her consciousness like a fishbone across the throat.

But ah, the compensations of her marriage. The opportunity to go forward with her music, the two summers of study at the Chicago Conservatory with Maestro Fantochi. How else could she ever have rated as a recital pianist? Technically at least, she could now be considered that. Her agent had managed to create a bit of demand for her afternoon services at women's clubs in the smaller towns of the state, occasionally in Illinois and Indiana as well.

Every November—at John Henry's expense, to be sure— she played a recital in a small hall in St. Louis, distributing tickets among her friends and her friends' friends. John Henry and Charley managed to fill a row or two at these occasions, Claudia and Brock, Clara and Clarabelle called into attendance. But Ed stubbornly demurred. It was one of the few occasions when Clara and Ed openly clashed.

"I don't see why we have to bear the brunt of these concerts alone, Ed. After all, she's your brother's wife, not mine. If anyone in the family should attend, it's you."

"It's a womanfolk's job," he would persist stubbornly. "Anchutz and I have puttering to do around the house."

Myra continued to build a local name for herself. Twice a week she taught at a girls' school in Kirkwood and once a week at Huntington Hall in South St. Louis. Her nominal earnings she presented to her mother.

John Henry had his overworked little witticism concerning this. "I thought I had married my wife in order to be supported by her in the style to which I had been accustomed. And what does she do? She supports everybody except her hubby."

Even Charley, who in the beginning had been stunned by this marriage, now entertained a certain pride in his sister-in-law. One of the two Steinway grand pianos, the finer in Myra's glassed-in studio, which she had built across the roof of the Georgian house, was a gift from him.

In her occasional interviews with the local press of the small towns in which she appeared Myra was given to stressing, "My first duty is to my husband. After that comes my profession."

If only, she sometimes dared to let herself think, John Henry were a bit more interesting.

Dear John Henry; he wasn't.

On the Sunday evening that Charley was seated in his drawing room, head in hands, Myra was playing a Chopin étude at one of the grand pianos, John Henry asleep on the couch, a newspaper over his face.

Chapter 7

WHAT A GOOD GIRL

OF ALL EVENINGS, CLARA DREADED MOST FOR CLARABELLE
to be unengaged on Saturdays and Sundays. She did not like
it too much in the case of Anchutz, but at least he was at
home by choice, working away down in the basement with
his father or with his friend Fred Kirsch, one of the young
men also employed in the shipping department of Henschen's.

Anchutz had quite a turn of the wrist for carpentry. The
window boxes across the front of the house were of his making. So were Clara's extension kitchen table and Rowdy's
fine big house in the back yard, large enough to contain three
instead of just the one fox terrier. It was Ed's proud boast
that his bed board for his arthritic back, priced fifteen dollars
at Stix Baer and Fuller's, Anchutz had made for less than
one dollar and fifty cents. He not only repaired their radio
and television sets, plumbing, roof leaks, but the neighbors'

40

as well. The kidney-shaped dressing table in Clarabelle's room, with the white organdy ruffle and candle brackets on each side of the mirror, he had fashioned for her birthday. Clara would have preferred that he spend some of this time "sparking" some nice girl, as she put it old-fashionedly.

This he did occasionally, but for the most part the twins were both home evenings.

But Clarabelle was there because there was no one to escort her out, and no girl wanted to rely steadily on a brother. What a good girl, Clara would have told you. Sweet, industrious. What a wife she was going to make some man. Old Mr. Gray, the lawyer Clarabelle had served as stenographer ever since she finished business school, doted on her. What a good girl! For that matter, never a day's trouble over either of her children, and when Clara compared them to Claudia or Brock—well, the less said, the better.

To be sure, Clara would concede grudgingly, but only to Ed, perhaps Claudia was prettier and Brock handsomer. How it happened, Clara could not understand, since Ed was by all odds the best-looking of the brothers. I must be the plain one, she would conclude ruefully, to make the difference.

Ed would pooh-pooh staunchly. Besides, looks were only skin deep, and to hear Clara talk you would think their kids were scarecrows instead of just nice-looking. Wouldn't trade them for five Claudias and Brocks.

Clara would not have, either, but just the same it hurt her to see Clarabelle, three years after her younger cousin Claudia had already been married and divorced, home evening after evening, unsought, unmarried, or accompanying her and Ed to a neighborhood motion picture or sitting down in the basement, watching the boys hammer and saw.

It hurt Clara so that sometimes she cried secretly in her clothes closet.

Chapter 8

TWO YEARS LATER

CLAUDIA AT TWENTY-SIX HAD ONE OF THOSE REMINDING faces. Someone like her hung hauntingly in the memory. The droll fact was that Claudia, full of knots inside her, nevertheless resembled the cherub in the lower left-hand corner of Murillo's madonna. The eyes blue and unclouded by those inner knots. The nose young as a child's. No matter how dead she sometimes felt within herself, that small uplifted face of hers, with its frame of sunny baby-fine hair, seemed new as dawn.

Divorced, childless, she continued to live in the boulevard home she had occupied during the brief period of her marriage to Frank Hagedorn, pitcher for the St. Louis Sunflowers.

Designed and originally occupied by an eminent architect, it was a period gem, outstanding on a boulevard of larger and more pretentious mansions. Frank, who at the time of their marriage was planning to retire from baseball in a season or two and enter an architectural firm, had resisted the purchase on the grounds of upkeep.

Charley, who in the beginning had not encouraged the marriage to a ballplayer, agreed with Frank, but deferred to his daughter's selection.

As it transpired, and as Frank had predicted, the high rate of taxes, the number of servants required, the general scale of living and entertaining, taxed his opulent salary to its limit. Claudia's income had to be requisitioned. Thereupon dissension reared its head. But not in the orthodox way.

Frank was for disposing of the house and moving into an apartment suited to his impending narrowing means as a junior in a prominent architect's offices.

"There will never be money comparable to what you are earning in baseball unless you accept my dad's offer to take you into one of his projects."

"You've known my intentions from the beginning, Claudia. I haven't swerved. But just you give me time, honey, and I'll be earning for you in architecture, more than I did in baseball."

"We can live on my money."

"As your gigolo. Fine!"

A barrage of such arguments, accusations, pleadings, tearful recriminations, reproaches, must have sunk into the woodwork of the lovely house, as Claudia clung to its luxuries.

Now, two years later, alone in that lovely house, her recriminations took place within herself, against herself.

To have tossed away what she had! Even her father had

long since conceded his error in judgment. Frank was a man!

On a small chaise longue in her little sitting room Claudia sat waiting. Not for Frank, but for her brother, prayerful that Brock could undo for her what she had done to herself and her life because she was the way she was.

Brock as usual was late, and the quiet Sunday evening seemed to stand stock-still, as if also waiting.

Her telephone kept ringing at short intervals. She had given orders in the kitchen that it was not to be answered. She was almost certain it was Richter. Fool, to have let herself get involved even to the extent of being frequently seen about with him, to say nothing of his unwanted but encroaching intentions. Why was she the way she was? Could it be, from what she understood was going on with her dad nowadays, that she too, now that she was free, was "letting go" that way? Nonsense. She had made a mistake, and, please God, not an irrevocable one. It was while she was waiting and praying that Frank would let her rectify it that Richter had helped whittle the terrible time away by giving her what Frank was refusing.

She contemplated the matter of Richter, of the Stove Foundry family. He was eleven years her senior, and some of the rumors about the slender, rather soprano-voiced fellow were strange. Not that she credited mere rumors, and her way of life and Richter's did seem in many ways to coincide. . . . If only Frank would move out of her heart as he had out of her house, other considerations would not seem so intolerable.

Brock had promised to arrive before six. She had set that hour in the event she should decide to allow Richter to come later. It was not often that she asked anything of Brock. It was not often, if ever, that she needed him. She needed him now!

Picking up the telephone receiver, she tried his office. Of course, no reply. Sunday. Next, the Metropolis Club, where he lived. Not in. Probably he was on his way.

She wondered as she sat how it was that she had refrained from enlisting his help all these two long years since her divorce decree had been handed down. But her overwhelming realizations regarding Frank had come gradually at first, and then suddenly swooped. Then the humiliations! Frank had not replied to her many successive letters. It was all she could do to restrain herself from making a personal visit to his South St. Louis home, where he was living with his parents. But, following his refusals by silence to her requests to see him personally, it was more than she dared risk.

After all it was through Brock, who had met Frank while they were in service in Korea, although in different outfits, that she had met her future husband.

She had it from Brock that occasionally he ran into Frank at the Athletic Club handball courts. He must make it his business to seek him out there and urge him to communicate with her. Once she had Frank face to face, something old and wonderful might come to life in him.

Those were Brock's footsteps coming up the front walk!

In some respects Brock was his sister's vigorously male and shining counterpart. People who remembered Polly as a girl said she had shone that way. To those who knew her only in later life this was inconceivable.

In a way Claudia and her brother were a pair of travelers

in good raiment, but with shabby interiors, walking a road that flashed with mirages.

Perhaps better than anyone, Brock's sister, who in so many respects was his equivalent in futility, knew him best, but not entirely. Like Charley, she sometimes suspected that his clumsily explained absences, his time lapses, indicated that he might be a solitary drinker. But, like her father, she had seldom seen him intoxicated, and then chiefly at functions where bourbon whisky or champagne in no great quantity could set him off.

At the sound of her brother's footsteps Claudia mixed him a bourbon on the rocks and without preamble met him full on.

"Brock, I want you to go to Frank for me. He won't see me."

Brock, whose postures were as relaxed as a cat's, collapsed his long body into a low chair, clasped his hands behind his head, feet out into the center of the room.

She walked around them to place the whisky beside him.

"I want Frank back, Brock."

"Are you kidding?"

"I was never more serious in my life. It may seem sudden to you, but it isn't to me. I made the mistake of my life, and I'm admitting it out loud now! It's been eating me for twenty-five terrible months. I want him back, on any terms."

"C.O.D.?"

"Don't be that way! It isn't often I've troubled you with my affairs. Listen to me with seriousness, if you have any."

"Okay, if I have any."

"I want him back, terribly."

"You don't make sense. It was cat-and-dog between you.

47

Didn't know a prince of a fellow when you had one. Even Dad conceded that and tried to hold you together."

"I must have been insane."

"You wanted a gigolo, and by mistake you got a man."

"Stop rubbing it in! I can't stand any more. I'm different now. I've learned my lesson. Just get him here, or me to him. Tell him I'm sick—anything."

"I did him one disservice, in throwing you together. I don't intend to do him another. Besides, he turns down a side street when he sees me coming. Guess we're a bad taste in his mouth."

"I'm desperate, Brock."

"I've been that since birth," he said laconically, flicking his cigarette ash.

"Well then, don't blame me, any more than I blame you for—never mind what."

"We'll leave my affairs out of this," he said darkly.

"We don't blame Dad for trying to get a little out of it for the years he's got left. Even with the old bag downtown somewhere they say he's living it up with. Mother was a virgin even after she married him and had us. I'll always think that's what cracked her up, if you ask me. I'm glad Dad is trying to get something out of it. I want something out of it too, even if you don't. I want Frank."

"And he wants out. Too bad, sis, that it didn't dawn on you in time how lucky you were to be married to a guy who didn't sit on his hands because he married a rich girl but to whom it meant a lot to do the earning for the family."

"But nowadays——"

"I know all about nowadays. That's fine when it works. Frank's way is old-fashioned, maybe. I went through the same thing in another way. She couldn't take me the way I was, and do her share of the compromising."

"Was it a crime to want to keep this roof over our heads, his as well as mine, instead of a hundred-dollar-a-month leaky one?"

"Yes, if it went so against your husband's grain."

"I could even understand it better if there had been another girl."

"He wanted kids. You wouldn't give him any. I heard you say as much."

"Only because I wanted a longer while to ourselves."

"That's what ails you and me, sis. Ourselves. It's none of my business whether you wanted kids or not, or why you didn't want them. But you're trying to make it my business, and I'm telling you in capital letters why I'm keeping out!"

She began to walk the floor, crying and not bothering to wipe away the wetness. "Goddamn it," she said through her pretty teeth. "Goddamn it," she repeated quietly but over and over again.

He watched her through his smoke. "There isn't a 'Goddamn' in Frank. They're all in you. I'll wager he's quiet now, and for all we know glad to be back living the kind of life his kind of person prefers. Hero stuff never went to that guy's head."

"Get him back for me, Brock. I'll be to him all the things I was not. It isn't too late for children. I want them now, believe me I do."

"You—running around town with this fellow Richter and in the same breath——"

"What do *you* know?" she flared angrily. "I'm running around because I'm running away from myself."

49

FAMILY!

He rose from the depths of his chair. "Damn it," he said, "I'd do it if Frank weren't so decent. But I can't and won't!" he flared and went out suddenly, angrily bitter and queasy because he could not bear to look upon anyone hurt.

Chapter 9

HER TWINS
WERE TWENTY-SEVEN

THAT SAME SUNDAY, REVEREND PHILLIP POLKINHORNE
and his mother were coming to dinner at the Ed Spragues,
following morning services at the Rock Church.

Against cooking odors, the windows were open from the
top, Clara's yellow curtains, newly laundered for this occasion, moving slightly.

Every touch had been twice and thrice administered, the
shining damask tablecloth smoothed, adjusted, readjusted,
a center bowl of pink carnations moved slightly right, then
slightly left.

The dining room, two decades in arrears of current décor,
was at its best. Clara, as her back and leg muscles were at-
testing, had shampooed the Axminster rug until its colors
leaped through the nap, and polished the dining-room "set."

"It's a pip, Mom," declared Anchutz, eying the scene that
was awaiting the pastor and his mother.

"You put a lot of 'pip' into it yourself, son, by washing

down the walls for me. I don't trust Clarabelle or your father on high places. And that polishing job you did on the front-room furniture certainly helps."

"I don't understand why you think our dining room is old hat, Mom. I like the china closet with the glass doors and dragon heads for feet. You can have that slick modern look that's all plate glass and chromium."

Clara knew why she felt about her dining room as she did. For herself it was all she could ask. But for Clarabelle she wanted it up-to-date, new and young. The old frame house, bat-gray, could subdue even the youth in the young, Clara reckoned. After all, her twins were only twenty-seven. They might have been livelier in a livelier house. They were staid children and it seemed to Clara that the good things in life were being achieved by young ones not so staid. She wanted hers to be gay and bring gay young people into the home as she had in her day. She wanted them to be as lovely in all eyes as they were in hers and Ed's. Most of all, she wanted them fulfilled as she and Ed were. Happily married, with children and homes. And here they were, still tied, as she tried to put it playfully, to her apron strings.

She loved having them there. Yet with her heart she did not want them there. Little use attempting to talk to Ed about such matters. He said such things as, "You women are the darnedest. Leave well enough alone. They'll get themselves married when the right girl and fellow come along. Didn't we? They suit me the way they are. When I look around, not any further than Charley's kids, I think we're pretty fortunate."

One impending circumstance that was life-size in Clara's mind did not seem to occur to Ed. Take this Sunday dinner.

Here was Reverend Phillip Polkinhorne, new in the community, young, unmarried, pastor of the church the Sprague brothers had attended since they were in knee pants. Did it so much as occur to Ed that over the months Clara had been diplomatically competing with the various mothers of daughters for this honor of entertaining Reverend Polkinhorne? No, it did not. Strictly speaking, protocol should have ordained that the Sprague families, considering their long-time identification with the church, be among the first to entertain the new pastor. But the edging for place among the mothers of eligible daughters had been so obvious that Clara, fearful that her sensitive Clarabelle might take notice of it, had been content to bide her time.

But well Clara knew that in the secret places of her heart, her daughter must be missing what life was not giving her. And why was it not? A dearer girl never lived, argued and argued Clara to herself. A wonderful little homemaker. A fine little "secretary," as Clara consistently designated her. Her little finger worth more than many of the looser-living girls who married and married well. If only Clarabelle could be rid of those thick-lensed glasses! Not even the fancy ones with rhinestone-studded frames helped.

Chapter 10

PLEASE, GOD . . .

WHAT CLARABELLE MIGHT HAVE FELT IN THOSE SECRET places of her heart, she kept there. Certainly she was not unaware that the Reverend Polkinhorne, personable and eloquent in the pulpit, was excitingly eligible, and that his mother, leaving home and husband in Davenport, Iowa, had come to West Grove to stand by until he could get settled.

Certainly she was aware of what "get settled" implied. Certainly she was experiencing those same thrills that raced down the spinal columns of the scores of other West Grove girls who were attending Sunday services and Wednesday-night prayer meetings with unprecedented regularity.

By tradition, a pastor, if he would fulfill his duties to their utmost, was expected by unwritten law to be married or to marry, in order that a mate might share certain duties inherent in his calling. Reverend Polkinhorne's predecessor, the late Reverend Beatty, had done it that way—married a

West Grove girl incidentally, the year he had taken over in that long ago when Ed and Clara were still childless.

Not even the waving antennae of Clara's intuitions could transmit to her the tenseness with which Clarabelle had sat through the months of Sunday mornings and Wednesday evenings and intervening social occasions. By day Reverend Polkinhorne, his sensitive face and resonant voice, hovered above her typewriter desk at the office, and filled the privacy of her bedroom at night.

She had yearned for this day, when Reverend Polkinhorne, going the congregation rounds, would finally reach them, and here it was, unreal, except that her father, his foot up on a kitchen chair, was snapping a flannel polishing cloth across his shoe, Anchutz running downstairs with two ties across his arm for advice as to choice, her mother, apron over her dark blue silk, opening the oven door to prod the long fork into the roast beef.

The last two or three times following services Reverend Polkinhorne had seemed not only to glance at her as she passed in the handshaking line on the church porch, but had seemed to hold her hand just a shade longer and with something faintly resembling a slight squeeze.

To recall it gave Clarabelle the sensation of descending too rapidly in an elevator.

Standing at the kitchen table, slicing carrots into crisp spikes to lie on a bed of cracked ice along with celery and black olives, Clarabelle glanced over her shoulder at her mother on her knees before the oven, her silk dress spanning her wide posterior.

Even though she would enter no discussion with her on the delicate subject of the young pastor, how well she knew the hopes that were tumbling through her mother's mind as she probed that roast. Time after time similar hopes had been slapped down, only to rise again. The young claims agent for an interurban bus company who had boarded a few houses down the street had asked her to motion pictures quite a few times, had her meet his parents at dinner in his home, and then moved away without even a farewell note.

Ken Miltonberger, a friend of Anchutz who played with him on the softball team of the Young Men's Christian Association, was the "son" in Miltonberger and Son's large retail hardware store in St. Louis. Clarabelle, escorted by Anchutz, had first met him at a "Y" dance. He subsequently took her to two more of the dances, had dinner at the Spragues several times, and on each occasion brought a pound box of chocolates which he devoured.

Clarabelle had already begun to glow, spent more time over her hair and nails, and shopped after office hours for a new blouse or pieces of costume jewelry. Clara said no word, but her heart was high. Neither Anchutz nor his father seemed to notice.

Then Ken's visits also suddenly ceased.

"Where is Ken these days?" inquired Clara of her son one evening, trying to keep her voice casual and not daring to glance at Clarabelle. "Doesn't he like our dinners any more?"

"Oh, didn't I tell you? His father is opening another store in Alton and he suddenly made up his mind to let Ken go there to manage it," replied Anchutz, his sister obviously not entering his mind.

Ed too munched away, unaware that a misery lay in Clara's heart and that Clarabelle was holding her last bit of food in her mouth for fear it would not go down. Humiliation, a kind of despair, gripped her. What do I lack? What is wrong with me? What, what?

Clarabelle never had reason to repulse the young men, because there were never advances. With surprising simplicity for a girl who had come to maturity in an era of increasingly free relations, even premarital, between the sexes, she wondered as she listened to the girls at the office why she had never been chased around a desk.

And now, once more, expectancy. The Reverend Polkinhorne. Beyond any previous dreams she had ever entertained, this time the fierce pain of love lived with her. That slight tightening of his handshake, his eyes turning ever so slightly in her direction as she walked away, were more, she felt almost certain, than hallucination.

"Please God," Clarabelle kept saying within herself as she moved the centerpiece on the table so that more of the carnations were before the plate of Reverend Polkinhorne. "Please God." She did not add, "Please God, what?" She was ashamed even in the presence of her innermost self.

Chapter 11

HALF A PASTOR

WALKING HOME FOLLOWING SUNDAY DINNER AT THE Spragues, the Reverend Polkinhorne's mother, who fell short of his shoulder, hooked her arm into his. She had weighed the same hundred and ten pounds all her adult life, was mother to eight sons, all living except one, a war casualty, and at sixty-nine had never experienced an illness.

Phillip was her only American-born child. The others had first seen light of day in the far-flung East during her husband's missionary days. Three of the sons were missionaries there now, and all except Phillip, her youngest, married.

It had been roots down for her sons, if not into American soil, at least into a family. The three in India had all taken American wives, the three living in the United States, two French and one Canadian. She was in West Grove with the unavowed hope of seeing her youngest and in many ways her dearest, although she would not admit it, take unto himself a mate, now that he was established in a flourishing parish.

"That Clarabelle Sprague is a mighty nice girl, son."

"She certainly is, Mother."

"And a mighty nice dinner, with her preparing a good part of it, at the home of mighty nice folks."

"Certainly was, Mother."

"I know a fine girl when I see one. Your brothers will testify to that."

"Indeed you do," he replied, as unctuously as if talking to a parishioner. As a matter of fact, his board had given him to understand, when his appointment was still in the discussion stage, that an unmarried pastor was little more than half a pastor.

It had been the same in his previous pastorates. But now, after what amounted to his apprenticeship years in very small communities, Phillip was ready.

Between him and Verna Wright, accomplished daughter of a Davenport surgeon, there had existed, over a high-tension period of about two years, one of those unspoken but understood engagements, his fraternity pin, her pledge.

Following the turnabout in Verna's affections, his mother had helped him through a bad period to a good recovery. But all of his urges had been awakened and slapped down, leaving him with more pain than even his mother realized.

This time he wanted to be quieter in his choice. It was honorable, he reasoned, for a man in his position to want to begin a home and family—well, with a girl he could like and respect. That was what he meant by quieter. He could now settle for that contentedly, wary of again letting go the full surge of his emotions.

59

". . . a mighty nice girl out of a mighty nice family. Real people, son. God lives in their house."

"Right you are, Mother."

"You know, I got to thinking over the little Eberhardt girl—Blossom, isn't it?"

"Yes."

"I know you've taken to her, but, funny thing, sweet and pretty as she is, in some ways she reminds me of—Verna. Not that I mean she and Verna are similar in character. Heaven forbid!" Mrs. Polkinhorne mentioned the name as if it had a bitter taste.

He did not say that part of the flash of attraction he had fleetingly experienced was just that similarity.

"It was just the way she widened her eyes, and the oval, saintlike little face, and all that fire . . ."

"A burned child should fear fire, Mother," he said in his bland white voice.

She patted his hand as they turned into the garden of the Pirner residence, where they were temporarily housed. "Nonsense. Your brothers George and Ronald both were singed before the lovely girls they finally married came along. You have the pick of West Grove and for that matter, the whole city of St. Louis. Take your time, son."

"I must be ripe for marriage, Mother, to be able to rationalize about it this way."

"I tell you that Sprague girl has qualities for a minister's wife. Friendly, capable, interested in church activities, and above all interested in a certain young reverend. It sticks out all over her, Phillip, plain as the nose on your face."

"She does grow on one."

"Exactly. I don't say she's a beauty. Not that she isn't nice-looking, but her real beauty is within."

"Let's not make your West Grove visit a shopping tour for—young ladies, Mother."

"Of course not. But if you should happen to make a choice while I'm here, I could go home to your father with wonderful news."

"A man doesn't decide those things overnight."

"Of course he doesn't, and I'm the last one to press you. But I like gray eyes that are wide apart and quiet. And give me a girl with long hair with those smooth mouse-colored braids around her head. I don't pretend that they're the prettiest color in the world."

"I don't believe I noticed."

"You've been noticing enough to inquire about her last Sunday morning on the church porch."

"Didn't I do the same about Blossom Eberhardt the Sunday before we went to dinner at her home? Didn't I do the same about Miss Jean Parker before we had dinner there? Remember, I'm relatively new in town, Mother."

"I'm glad you didn't take to the Parker girl, Phillip, no matter how big and fine their home and all that goes with her. You just take your time, son—about this whole business."

"I wish God hadn't broken the mold when He made you, Mother."

They entered the hallway where a lamp with a low-watt bulb had been left burning. The mother of the Reverend Polkinhorne stood tiptoe and reached up to place both hands on her son's shoulders before kissing him good night.

"There is nothing wrong, Phillip, about seeking carefully

for the right woman. It is the most important selection you will ever be called upon to make. Your old mother was wished on you. You had no choice."

"Thank God for that and for you," he said and kissed her.

Chapter 12

HE NEEDED TO WALK
AND THINK

CHARLEY, EMERGING FROM HIS CONTEMPLATIVE HUNCH, TOOK up his hat from the hall table and ignoring his car, which stood in the driveway, walked out into a calm and darkening evening. There were stars and more than a hint of frost. He turned up his collar and began to stride in the direction of a bus stop.

He was recalling, by rather remote association, the case of John Henry, immediately preceding his marriage to Myra. It had required intervention into John Henry's "indiscretion" to disentangle him. He recalled the woman's name, so long forgotten. Willie-Sue. It seemed to come back to him on a whiff of her strong scent. The matter had been liberally and quietly adjusted.

Not that you could speak of Virgie and Willie-Sue in the same breath. Great Scott, no! But as the bus rumbled him down into Virgie's area, he could trace the association of ideas. Willie-Sue had lived in this same neighborhood. He had called on her several times during the settlement between her and John Henry.

Well, thank God, Virgie was nobody's business but his own. As a matter of fact, he was not even sure that her business was any of his business. He knew her pretty well, and yet if you broke it down, how little he actually knew! What was more, he did not care. He wouldn't swap her little finger for Myra, Clara, or the whole kit and kaboodle of them.

He had met her conventionally enough, although in what for him was an unaccustomed haunt. Isaiah Cronin, an acquaintance, sales manager for a brewery, had introduced her while she was enjoying pig's knuckles and sauerkraut with him in a bar and grill.

But what explanation did he owe anyone, now that poor Polly was gone? He had kept his marriage almost inviolate over all the long years. More than many a man would have done, he protested loudly and frequently to himself.

By heaven, now that he was alone nobody was going to tell him how to run his life. A man of his age and, yes, a man of his urges had a right to live up the years that were left to him. Live them up to the hilt. Get no thanks if he didn't. One queen of a girl!

In no time at all he was walking up the outside stairway to Virgie's apartment. In the loose white negligee she wore about the house, usually belted-in for guests, she sat brushing away at the rough coat of the downstairs grocer's old Scotch terrier, Judo, who visited her sporadically.

Charley could not know to what extent, on just this chance that he might thus walk in on her, it had required managing for her to be alone. She had maneuvered it on no more than the hope that he might come. Hermie Levinne, whose neckwear factory was facing bankruptcy, had brought his doldrums to her and she had eased him homeward. The "boys" must learn that they could no longer drop in, except by telephone appointment.

Also, Isaiah Cronin had sent in half a case of beer and a whole salami, with a view to following up the evening with a visit, but she had denied him on the same off chance that Charley might come.

The boys, accustomed as they were to forgathering for the warmth and sympathetic ear of Virgie, no longer stretched their legs out into the center of her living room as if sunning themselves. Not even Alan Bevin, son of a congressman, brother-in-law of an admiral, Virgie's "poor pilgrim," as she termed him, a sodden remnant of a man who, ten years before, had been district attorney in a large Southern city.

It is doubtful if Charley realized any of this. Arriving without warning, he relaxed into the deep curve of a chair that already, by unspoken designation, was his. What a woman! Her place fitted him like an old shoe.

He did not attempt to analyze it, but ever since Cronin, whom he knew to be a man of family, had introduced him to Virgie, he had assiduously avoided him. He no longer lunched at the Downtown Club. Cronin lunched there. From Cronin he could doubtless have learned more about Virgie. But he knew what he knew, and that was sufficient.

Virgie, who drank only in moderation and then chiefly beer, placed a cool bottle of Cronin brew beside Charley. Also a moderate imbiber, he drank slowly, regarding her over the foam.

"I like to come here," he said.

She was cheerful and without wile. "I like to have you

65

come, Charley. There's a long latchstring on my door for you."

If he asked of himself, And for how many others? he did it without rancor. He could have sworn to this much: here was a good woman.

"Funny thing. Don't know that I ever thought about it before. But I begin to feel myself a lonely man in a big house. It's come over me only since my wife passed away. That might seem only natural, except, as you know, she hadn't been living at home for fifteen years."

"That isn't a funny thing, Charley. While she lived, you just sort of felt bound."

"Must have. Something holds a man with a sick wife, even if she's sick in the head."

Virgie was moved to rise and place another cushion behind his neck. "You sit and relax while I whip together some supper. I've a sirloin, your cut and as thick as your fist, and my French-fries are ready to drop into the grease."

"I'll take you down to Kittner's for supper," he offered weakly.

"Give me a rain check," she said.

"You always say that," he protested more weakly.

"Isn't it nicer here?" she asked, when they were presently seated before a card table spread with a lace cloth, the steaming scents rising and filling the room with coffee odors and the faint raciness of the garlic with which she had lightly brushed the toasted French bread.

He closed his eyes and sniffed as if inhaling garden fragrance. "You must have learned to cook in heaven."

"I learned it in my mother's boarding house for hungry dock workers," she said laconically.

"My mother was also a good cook, and we kept boarders too."

"That must be one reason why we feel so at home together."

"We do that, don't we?"

"Like I've known you a lifetime."

He felt that way in spite of the fact that actually he knew so little of her. He glanced about. There was a jar of pipe tobacco on the table beside him. A closet door was standing open, revealing a man's raincoat and a slouch hat on a shelf. His eyes rested on a framed wall photograph of a heavy-set young sailor in United States uniform.

"I haven't told you about Grant yet, Charley. He's my son. He was thirty-six last week."

"You don't look even twenty-six yourself, Virgie."

"I'm fifty-three next April, Charley, so you can figure how old I was when I had Grant. Not quite sixteen. I haven't seen him, it will be eight years."

"How come?"

"He was mustered out of the Navy some years ago. Stayed over in Australia. Met a girl from Melbourne, daughter of one of those tycoon ranch owners."

"Those fellows are bigger than Texas."

"I'll say. My boy, who had salt water in his veins like his father before him, now runs one of his father-in-law's ranches that sounds like you could set New Jersey down in the middle of it!"

"Doesn't he send you——"

"You know how it is," she interrupted, anticipating him. "After all, Grant only works there. From what he gives me to understand between the lines, they are fine people but a little strait-laced in—in certain ways. You get me?"

"I get you."

"With a wife and a father-in-law—well, life being the way it is, that's the way it is."

Charley did not ask about Grant's father.

It was enough that here was the kind of woman with whom you could sit back and let her ready talk, often humorous, sometimes a little raffish, offbeat, bold, flow along, and her ministrations soothe you. Another cushion, a drink, a smoke, a lampshade tilted away from your eyes.

It did not matter much what she said. Virgie's laugh had the same down-under throaty quality as her voice. She could tell one of her lusty stories and whack a man's knee out of her own enjoyment of it. She had a kind of self-intoxication that transmitted itself. Charley usually returned home feeling heady with nothing more than Virgie.

He liked to watch her cross a room, her posterior wagging. Her slight heaviness intensified her femaleness. Strange how the manner in which this woman moved could affect him! He had never noticed it before. How had Polly moved in the years when it would have mattered? This one moved as if she were made of music. There was a woman, through and through.

Sometimes when the telephone in the hallway rang he would pick up, but with nothing more than idle curiosity, tidbits of what went on in her way of life. "No, Jess, didn't I tell you? The boys don't meet here any more for cards. I shooed them all down to Kittner's Bar, where they can hire that little side room out of money from the kitty." Or: "Well, Roody, when did you get to town? Sorry, fellow, I've had to shorten the old latchstring. . . . Give my regards to yourself. You'll find the fellows nowadays down at Kittner's Bar . . . sorry, fellow . . ."

He could scarcely help overhearing. As a matter of fact, he did not exactly want to overhear. For the first time, this particular evening she returned to the room from one of the telephone calls, explaining. "That was one of the old crowd. Somehow or other since you came I have shooed most of them away."

He felt excited and warmed. Obviously he was in her thoughts. "I don't want to be the cause of chasing away your friends."

She rumpled his hair as she passed his chair. "Oil and water don't mix."

He captured her hand and held it clamped to the top of his head. "Which am I, oil or water?"

"Oil, because you're more valuable."

For the first time, and unmindful of her inaccuracy, he spoke words almost amorous. "Virgie, there is something about you and me that makes it right."

"I'm glad you said that, but I don't hold you to it."

"Why?"

"I guess because I'm that way."

"But what if I'd like to be held to it? Come around here and sit on my lap," he said, releasing her hand.

She obeyed matter-of-factly. He felt her soft bigness, which he thought beautiful.

"I'd like to do something for you, Virgie," he said, as much as anything to steer himself away from what he felt crowding to his lips. "I've been eating off you, using your

69

house space and company a good while now. I think it's about time I began to reciprocate."

"Charley, you owe me just exactly nothing. I don't do for nobody—for anybody that I don't get real pleasure out of doing."

"I'm rich, honey. I'm not going to feel it."

"That don't mean you owe me any more than anybody else."

"Know what I'd like to give you?"

"No, because I've never thought about having it, and that's God's gospel, so help me."

"I'd like to give you a Cadillac, its care and feeding thrown in." Why not, he argued quickly to himself. What was he saving for? Nobody needed him.

"Charley, don't make me laugh. What would I do with a Cadillac? I couldn't drive a kiddie car."

"Did I say anything about not throwing in a chauffeur as well?"

She lay back against him, full of laughter. "Wouldn't I cut a figure? I don't care any more for just riding around for the sake of riding around than you do. I notice you come by bus most of the time."

"That doesn't mean you should. I want to give you something. Not that I can give you enough to express my appreciation for all you've given me in wonderful dinners and everything in the way of consideration and kindness."

"Stop it or you'll make me cry."

"And at a time when I most needed it."

"I'm glad I've been able to be around and share bad times with you."

"Not that I've ever pretended, Virgie, that the going of the wife meant bad times. It was a release for her and, let's face it, for me."

"The bad times, Charley, must be recalling the good times you had before—she took sick."

"Something in that," he said, lifting her fingers one by one. "The girl I married and the woman who died—good God—I sometimes wonder, can they have been one and the same?"

"Don't think of it, Charley."

"You've kept me from it, Virgie."

"I'm glad, and remember, I don't want a Cadillac for it."

"Then tell me what you want. Name it."

"Just exactly what we've got, Charley," she said, squirming around on his lap so that they were face to face. "I've never had anything in my life as nice as this. Men like you don't often come the way of a woman like me."

He felt a rush of feeling and slid her off his knee. He needed to get out and get going. Walk and think and walk and think.

Chapter 13

VIRGIE SCOGAN
AND CHARLEY SPRAGUE!

Following Charley's departure, Virgie turned off the lamps. It was pleasant to ruminate in the soft dark, an old habit of hers.

Virgie Scogan and Charley Sprague! Fantastic that he should be her—friend. Charley Sprague and Virgie Scogan.

Why should it be fantastic? Why had she let the ordered life slip by her? Indeed, she had never even touched it, any more than her mother before her. She was as tethered to her way of life as Charley, during the lifetime of his incarcerated wife, had been to his.

In spite of herself, she was feeling with a kind of pain how little life had offered to her through the years.

Had the fault been hers, or the almost unmentionable conditions of her so-called home?

Mac, her ex-longshoreman, had married her in a stupor. Two years later he died in one, leaving her Grant, over two thousand dollars in large denominations, which she did not know he had, stuffed into a woolen sock, and a five-thousand-dollar life-insurance policy which she had urged and kept up out of part-time earnings as waitress in a diner.

When Virgie awoke at night with wet eyes, as she did sporadically, she knew she had been crying in her sleep, for love's labors' lost. Strange that this boy of hers should have run off from the opulence of her love, the way his father had so often threatened before his death.

She had never before been close to the side of life Charley represented. Nice people. Business and personal status.

Alan Bevin had once belonged there. But she had come to know him only at the sodden stage of his wasted career. All her life that side of the coin had seemed to turn its face upward to her. Soiled lives, doomed people. Those who despaired, tugging at her compassion.

That compassion ran forward now to meet Charley Sprague, who might not be needing it at all. What was possessing her? Men were not new to her. Where were her hard-earned knowledges?

Past the years when such thoughts any longer crowded her mind for place, she nevertheless found herself thinking in terms of her desirability. Had she any kind of that allure left? Charley had, where she was concerned.

Every meeting seemed to bring him closer, but never a suggestion beyond the stroked hair, the lap, the occasional kiss. Had desire to sleep with her ever stirred him?

In the world of men in which she grew up her desirability had been the bane of her girlhood. But now, suddenly, she was mourning her youth. . . .

Steps on the outside staircase were not alarming to Virgie, even when they staggered. She switched on a lamp and watched the door slowly open. A man lurched in, his sway unmistakable, the skin of his gray face stretched so tightly that the skull strained through. He had the baggy body-bigness of one who has lost much weight; his shapeless clothing hung that way. A long, lean cadaver of a man.

Before she could rise, he fell beside her chair, put his face into her lap, and began the easy tears of befuddlement.

"Thank God you're back. I'm cold, Virgie, through and through."

"I'll get you a blanket, Alan."

"No, no. Blankets won't warm my kind of cold. Warm me, Virgie."

She had heard this repetitiously throughout the several years he had periodically come staggering to her, sobbing after long unexplained absence, for her comfort, her largesse. She let him rest his cheek against her knees, his bony back rising and falling.

"Alan, where have you been these months?"

"In hell, Virgie."

"Have you been far or just around the river front?"

He beat his fists against his forehead. "My brother-in-law, the Admiral, and my sister——" he began, fumbling as the continuity of his thought snapped. "You remember, they were off me for good, they said, after the last time. Well, they came up again with an idea for another try—another try—another——"

"Yes, Alan, your sister and the Admiral decided to give you another chance?"

"The Admiral sent me a plane ticket and a new suit to join them in Newport News—a doctor there—a new kind of

shock treatment. They wanted to try again—to try again—as
if there were any use——"

"And?"

"With the plane ticket in my pocket, I could feel it burning through, burning my throat, my gizzard. I didn't want
it to happen. I wanted help, and you were gone, Virgie."

"You pawned it, Alan, and the suit?"

"On the way up the stairs to you to help me not to do it,
I could see you and a middle-aged heavy-set fellow through
the window. He was the kind I am ashamed to face. I didn't
want to make you ashamed too. I went away, but I was burning with the fire——"

"Alan, Alan, you didn't!"

"I did. Hocked the suit and redeemed the plane ticket——"

"You drank them instead?"

"I must have, but somewhere along the way I think I was
gypped out of some of it."

"You don't remember?"

"I remember the judge. He gave me ten days to get sobered
and cleaned up. I asked for thirty. He gave them to me.
That's where I've been until three weeks ago."

"And then, Alan?"

"I met a fellow down near the levee who was paying fifty
dollars for old passports. I let him have mine—I was burning,
Virgie."

"Alan, you can go to jail for that! You surely know they
doctor them and sell them for illegal entries into the
country."

"I know—I know. Before I became district attorney,
I handled many such cases. Don't go into it. Help me, quiet
me down. Slap my face, hard. . . . Harder, harder. Give me

back your lap. Let me lie here. Die here. God must be the devil, not to let me die——"

"Alan, Alan, how can any of us help you? Must we keep failing?"

"Don't ever give me money again, Virgie. For God's sake, don't."

"I won't, Alan. Come, I'll walk you over to Bill's Hotel for Men. Get to bed and sleep it off. Then we can plan a new try. I'll fix you coffee so you can walk to Bill's."

"Let me rest here, Virgie. Don't send me to Bill's. I'm too beat to make it."

"Coffee will fix you up."

She slid herself away from him, but he followed.

"Don't leave me alone——"

"I'll be back with your coffee."

He leaned his head against the frame of the kitchen door and began to descend slowly, as if his legs would no longer sustain him.

"Let me lie down."

She replaced the coffeepot on its shelf and led him into her small room, removed the costumed dolls and pink coverlet from the bed, and sat him down on the edge.

"I'll take off your shoes," she said, beginning to unlace them.

"Rub the soles of my feet, Virgie. They're burning up, like me."

She dragged off the socks. There was fastidiousness left in him, and he groaned at their holes. She did not recoil but after rubbing them briskly stretched him out and covered him.

"Help me, Virgie."

"Lie down a bit and then we'll go to Bill's." She clicked out the light and started to tiptoe from the room.

"No, no, no! Don't go!" he cried, springing up. "Don't leave me. Stay. Hold me. Warm me—lie down beside me——"

She laid herself atop the coverlet, soothing him as one would a child.

A kind of hopelessness smote her. She had worked hard with Alan, and yet each time this happened, the need to try once more gripped her, as apparently it had his sister and the Admiral.

He lay with his face against her body. She held him so, long into the night, as if he were the small boy this soiled, defeated man incredibly must once have been.

77

Chapter 14

PRIVATE AND FORBIDDEN
THOUGHTS

Brock Sprague once said of his cousin Clarabelle Sprague, that she looked like the sort of girl who bathed under a sheet.

Up in her room beneath the eaves of the pleasantly shabby house she had occupied almost all the years of her life, Clarabelle, figuratively speaking, was thinking thoughts under a sheet. She was ashamed of them. She did not want them. They kept coming. They had to do with her and her pastor, the Reverend Polkinhorne.

In the lawyer's office where she was employed, these thoughts did not seem so reprehensible. But once she reached the privacy of her room and thought them in bed, she could almost feel herself blushing for herself.

It was raining, the cold steady November way, and the patter on the roof, which usually she enjoyed, went unnoticed. She and the Reverend had spent the evening together at a neighborhood motion picture. She had hoped for a ro-

78

mantic drama while seated beside him, but the picture had to do with wildlife in Africa.

After the showing, he had returned home with her for coffee and a slice of the four-tier chocolate cake she had baked the evening before.

It was the third such evening within the month, to say nothing of the Sunday mornings and Wednesday evenings when she could either look down at him from the choir loft, where she sang frail but not unmusical soprano, or up at him from a pew.

Three members of the congregation besides herself made up the choir. From that high vantage she could gaze down upon the Reverend at the altar. His hair rolled back from his brow in a wave. Even that was one of the thoughts that held excitement.

At night, more private and forbidden thoughts came out like mice. His knee had been against hers, true, without pressing, as they sat side by side in the darkness of the theater. The Reverend's breathing was in that darkness, the warmth of his body close to hers; his hands, carefully to himself, with little islands of hair on the backs of them, were breathing.

All of that she was feeling up in her little room, and more. And now, to her continuing sense of shame, he was lying, in her imagination, full length in her arms, her lips pressed into that wave of his hair, its smell masculine.

Frustrated old maids were supposed to have secret thoughts like this. Well, going on twenty-eight, what else was she but an old maid? Except that now—who knows— perhaps? Even though her parents made no mention of it, the new tensions in the house stemmed from awareness that she was being singled out for occasional escorting by the young Reverend.

Only Anchutz went his way unplumbed, puttering away his evenings in his basement workshop, tinkering, with his father, at a short-wave radio, or sprawling on a couch, head low, legs high, watching television Western dramas or baseball.

This oblivion of his had innocently been the source of some agonizing incertitudes.

One evening at the dinner table, Anchutz, declining a second baked potato, remarked casually, "Sorry, Mom, no more, full up. Ran into the Reverend just now, living it up with the Eberhardt doll at the soda fountain in Gregg's Drugstore. Nothing would do but I join them and split my appetite with a banana split. Anything cooking between those two?"

Clarabelle, her throat suddenly blocked against swallowing, pushed on with her meal, the food going down painfully, her forced conversation incessant.

But the following morning the Reverend had telephoned, had come to dinner that evening, and then the two of them had gone on to the pictures—and now again, tonight, just one week later.

He liked her! She felt it in her bones. Else why with all his invitations should he choose to come to dinner three weeks in succession in a home so much simpler than those of most of his congregation's? He likes me!

For all I know, he takes Blossom Eberhardt just to keep all the wigwags in town from wigwagging. I'm more his type. A minister's wife can't change the color of her hair every few months and smoke cigarettes the way Blossom does. Please

God, make it not Blossom. I'm the one he needs. I'll live only for what is good and right for him. He'll never regret it. It isn't wrong to want to sleep with the man you love and wake with the man you love and creep inside the man you love.

She covered her face with her hands.

Chapter 15

HAIR ON HIS CHEST

Anchutz had brought his friend, Fred Kirsch, one of the boys who worked beside him down at the firm, home with him for dinner.

After the meal they disappeared into the basement, where they were constructing a feeding trough for their joint enterprise, a pigeon house on Fred's roof.

Anchutz's basement, where he spent most of his evenings tinkering, was a world of his own. In addition to the paraphernalia of carpentry and electrical equipment, were a cot with an army blanket in one corner, a two-burner gas ring, a shelf containing a miscellany of plates, cups, and saucers, an old icebox which the boys had rejuvenated, and a small table that once had been in the upstairs front hall.

Between them, Clara and Clarabelle kept the icebox stocked for those evenings he brought home friends. Cold tongue, hard-boiled eggs, leftovers from the family table, usually part of a freshly baked cake, and always chilled soft drinks and beer.

On the rare evenings when some of "the fellows" brought girls, a Victrola needled dance tunes well on into midnight.

Clara occasionally urged, "Anchutz, haven't any of those nice boys and girls you bring to the house every once in a while older brothers whom you might also invite, for your sister's sake?"

"Maybe. I'll find out."

He never did. Clarabelle's problem simply would not penetrate. Cripes, a girl knows when she's ready to get married without any fixers trying to meddle in. Cripes, what gives girls the marriage jitters?

Anchutz and Fred sometimes discussed topics related to kindred matters.

This night, the pigeon trough completed, Fred launched forth, as they sat over tongue sandwiches and beer.

"Don't you ever get ants in your pants, Anch?"

"What's the idea, ants in my pants?"

"Itchings to go places. Do things. Change jobs."

"One job is about as good as another."

"That's what you say. I want to get places. I've got ambish."

"For what?"

"To make money, get married, have kids. Don't you ever think of things like that?"

Anchutz crinkled his face in cogitation. "Working at Henschen's isn't so bad. They've got a good pension system. They keep you on as long as the law allows. The bosses are okay. What more do you want? Look at my dad. When he's retired, he'll be sitting pretty."

83

"What's sitting pretty about it? Forty years' service and enough to exist on when you're old. Go tell your old man to put a bonfire under you."

"Get one under yourself."

"I've already got one. That's why I'm going to lickety-split it for something better than shipping clerk, instead of turning into one of their forty-year dray horses."

"You mean like my dad?"

"You said that, I didn't."

"Who's holding you back, if you're so loaded with ambish?"

"You know darn well. I've got a mother to help support and I can't jump reckless. But take it from me, no thirty or forty years in a rut not much better than a grave, and all for the magnificent hundred-dollar-a-month pension when I'm sixty-five. Your dad deserves better than that."

"If that's what you mean by ants in pants, my dad and I haven't got them. We're not a family with the itch."

"Your uncles have it, and see where it got them. I suppose you wouldn't want to be in their shoes."

"Maybe and maybe not."

"They can do big things for you."

"Says you."

"I'd like to see myself with that much power in my family."

"We prefer to run under our own power."

"Don't you want anything out of life except what you're getting?"

"What makes you think that the best things out of life are only the ones you can taste, see, and smell?"

"I'll settle for them. Don't you even want girls you can taste and see and smell?"

"Sure I like girls."

"You don't go steady. You don't even go in for an occasional he-man night on the town, do you? I mean all night."

"Suppose I don't?"

"Fellows are fellows. They need a floozy now and then to calm them down."

"Suppose I don't need calming?"

"Then that's what ails you. It's not natural not to. You're too calm."

"You're trying to tell me I'm not natural. What's not natural about liking to have fellows around in a natural way? I notice you show up here pretty regularly, especially on the nights Dad comes down with us to work on the radio."

"Sure, I like your dad. Sure, I like to fool around with ham radios and make dates with girls across the ocean."

"Girls. Girls. Don't you think of anything else?"

"You said it! It's unnatural if you don't. How else do kids get born to keep the world going?" Suddenly Fred looked at his friend, his eyes seeming to move closer together. "You mean you like fellows better than girls?"

"Sure. Less shenanigans. A fellow comes at you straight, instead of all curves and curlicues."

"You'd better not tell that to anybody else but me, kid; they might think things."

"What?"

"You can't be that dumb. Haven't you ever wanted to even kiss a girl?"

"Sure I have. What's it to you?"

"Haven't you ever laid one?"

"Cut it out, will you?"

"You're the kind of guy plays his cards close. I come out with it. I'll bet you could take me to more places in this town than I can take you, and believe you me, that would be going some."

That remark proved a face-saver for Anchutz. "Where do you think I've been all my life?" he replied cryptically.

"Atta boy. That's the stuff. Be yourself."

Anchutz smiled a little wryly, trying to keep the cryptic in his expression.

"Want to hear one about the pilot who made a forced landing on the roof of a whorehouse in Istanbul?"

Anchutz did not. But he loosened his collar and opened his shirt as far down as the hair on his chest.

"Shoot," he said.

Chapter 16

WHAT DID JOHN HENRY
THINK ABOUT?

EACH FRIDAY, EXCEPT WHEN ONE OF HER PIANO RECITALS prevented, which was not too often, Myra went home. Once John Henry had queried with what for him amounted to irritability. "What do you mean, going *home?* Aren't you at home here?"

"You know well and good what I mean, John Henry," she said, knowing that he did not. "Going home to Mama" was just a way of saying going home to her people. But subconsciously he did understand what she meant.

Over the years of their marriage he had been in that home eighteen times—that is, on each of his mother-in-law's birthdays—carrying the gift which Myra had purchased for him, sitting on the edge of his chair, sniffing at the alien air.

It was redolent with the smells that emanated from some kind of fish he could not at first identify, mingled with garlic and the bakeshop odor of those heavy round loaves of black bread sold by the pound in delicatessens.

When Myra returned from her visits to her mother she brought those odors back with her, but faintly, so that they evaporated quickly. On a trip to New York City he and Myra had taken a conducted tour. In the ghetto area there came those smells, Jewish fish, Jewish bread, Jewish people.

So every Friday evening Myra went home to her Jewishness. That was all right with him. But it did not make any the less a kind of strangeness which he thought about only on these occasions when Myra said she was "going home," or when he visited his mother-in-law in the stuffy little house on School Street, where the large crayon portraits on the walls were of men in black beards and skullcaps.

He liked his mother-in-law, but even after the years, he still found it difficult to understand her accent. But she plied him with sweet wine and cake, and held up her knotted hands for him to better understand the arthritis that plagued her much of the time.

Myra had long since abandoned the hope of ever removing her mother from the little house in which she herself had been born and to which her mother clung like fungus. John Henry had been generous, installing air conditioning and a Deepfreeze, designed more to keep the housemaid, whom Myra had insisted upon, satisfied than for the old lady, who eschewed them.

She stood in a certain awe of her son-in-law, but pride in her daughter's wealthy marriage was ever to be subordinated to a secret anguish. Her sole living child married to a *goy*. A gentile. Mrs. Goldonsky was grateful that her husband had not lived to see it. It was bad enough in the eyes of her friends and her sister in Tel Aviv, who had remained back in Warsaw for ten terrible years to face pogroms and worse, until the miracle birth of a new state of Israel.

As a matter of fact, Myra had sometimes marveled at her own ruthlessness in making this marriage during her mother's lifetime. But a girl supporting her mother and herself by giving piano lessons can be swept off her feet, if not by love, by the blessed event of a first offer of marriage, and that a sound one.

By now, there was something of genuine love in her heart for John Henry. They enjoyed interdependability, each imbued with enough of deep inner loneliness to give cause for gratitude for having one another.

Except for the little old lady in the black wig in downtown St. Louis, Myra had no reason for regret. The long years when a living for the family had to be wrested from the little store and newsstand opposite a public-school building, her own struggle for the settlement-house music lessons and ultimate free scholarship, still stood life-size in her memory.

Now she had a good man; she had wealth; she could do for her mother. In addition, she had the matchless compensation of being able to afford piano recitals, at her own expense, if need be.

In addition, she was frequently moved to turn over her small stipend, out of a sense of gratitude for a recital engagement, to a charity or back to the organization which had engaged her.

Buttressed by the delayed realization that she had not the musical stature for the concert stage, and her sense of frustration on the wane, it was more than ever a saving circumstance to be secure in her marriage.

Nevertheless, her piano remained her balm. She played

Bach not too well but as if it were a prayer. On trains or planes, she would pore over a score of Mozart or Brahms, oblivious to surroundings. This immense absorption resulted in a kind of attitudinizing at the keyboard, which, to some, bordered on the ridiculous.

When Myra played a Chopin étude, her eyes closed, her head tilted back, and her face became a theater for the display of her emotions.

Nevertheless, as she grew older, the atavism of eager return to her beginnings was manifesting itself. This had little to do with John Henry.

Following the initial shock of John Henry's marriage, the Spragues had come to regard her as the exotic boast of the family, critical only of the little recital tours which took her out of the home. They scrupulously attended her annual St. Louis public performances and distributed complimentary tickets among their friends. If the critics flayed, as they usually did, the family remained undaunted in its admiration for its accomplished member.

In the beginning the cleavage of the Ed Spragues had bothered Myra. Why need it be so? But John's keep-out-of-such-matters policy had been to the new bride a rebuff, relegating her to the outer periphery of the Spragues.

But after all, she reasoned, the separateness of her brother-in-law Ed and his family was no affair of hers. That was just the way it often was with the "gentiles," in contrast to the manner in which "her people" usually clung together like clusters of bees. Her own family, for instance.

As far back as she could remember, money and clothing out of the meager earnings of the little store had gone back to Warsaw and later to Tel Aviv, as well as to a distant relative in Peoria, Illinois, confined in a nursing home for the aged.

When younger, Myra had taken all this for granted. But now the Friday nights, then little more than a ritualistic duty to be fulfilled for her parents' sake, were more and more becoming nostalgic and tugging memories.

Seated opposite John Henry in the midst of dinner in their spacious surroundings, a rush of longing would recurringly overtake her for another table, candlelit for the Sabbath Eve, in a room so small that had it contained the table at which she and John Henry were seated, there would have been no aisle for passing.

Sundays, she accompanied John Henry to Rock Church, where he continued to function as usher, her prayers there, Jewish. Nights she said a silent Jewish prayer.

To be sure, there were times when John Henry, so far as compatibility of interests were concerned, seemed as flabby and tasteless as the foods she had learned to have served, or to prepare herself.

John Henry doted on what she termed "American dishes" —fried chicken, boiled ham, Boston baked beans, pies, especially the latter. He was also especially fond of lobster. They would come by air on special order from Maine, wrapped in wet seaweed and still squirming. Usually on lobster nights Charley Sprague came to them or vice versa. Crustaceous foods were forbidden by the dietary laws by which she had been reared. Her aversion to them contributed to the feeling of strangeness in an alien world that was occasionally beginning to overtake her.

John Henry, without intention, would twist and tighten this feeling. He had a way of referring to the Hebrew people which somehow set her apart from him. Even though she had not observed the dietary laws since her marriage, this kind of reference embarrassed her. "Sure you don't want one of these lobster claws, Myra? I'll dig it for you. . . . No? Funny thing about the Jewish people. Take Eisenberg, on the Board of Trade. That fellow don't observe the kosher laws any more than you do. But he just can't eat ham, any more than you can eat lobster. Goes against the grain of Jewish people, I guess."

The Jewish people. The Jewish people. These were the times she felt unbearably apart from Christians. Only you didn't label them "the Christian people."

But in the main John Henry was good to her and for her. It might be said they were good for one another. As a matter of fact, her sporadic absences from home seemed to rankle chiefly in Charley.

"She is a good girl," John Henry would invariably retort when his older brother recurringly remarked on the absences.

"You're right there, but there are plenty who play the piano as well as she does who don't have to run out on the home to do it."

"She's an artist and a good girl in one."

"Oh, you've got a good woman, no matter what her creed. You can be thankful for that much."

John Henry's reactions were slow, but something kept dangling in his mind—"no matter what her creed." That was a dig, if you asked John Henry. Why bring that up? Had they not agreed from the beginning that if there were children she would defer to John Henry's choice of their religious education, but only after her mother's death? That was fair enough, Charley had sanctioned at the time. Charley liked Myra, but dig he would.

In like manner, it disturbed John Henry to have himself pointed out as the Sprague brother who had married a Jewish girl.

If Myra felt any of all this, it was well laid away beneath the surface where she stored the pleasant contemplations of her Friday evenings.

Sometimes Myra felt herself wondering, What on earth does John Henry think about, all day, all evening? A little baseball, a little quail-hunting with Charley, golf? None of these was an engrossing hobby. Like his brother, politics seemed to concern him only when his immediate interests were concerned, chiefly tax legislation. As for business, fortunately for John Henry, his affairs were entirely under Charley's domination. With no decisions to make, what initiative he might have developed had long since gone flabby.

Yet his unlined face seemed to indicate that John Henry liked it that way. Meeting each day's trivia with good nature, he lacked the desire to vary routine or travel from it. In vain Myra placed steamship, railroad, and plane folders in his way. "Someday," was his invariable comment, "someday we'll see the world."

What did John Henry think about . . . ?

Considering that his background, his church life, and what business life he had were all out of Myra's domain, the degree of their compatibility was remarkable.

93

Chapter 17

SOMETHING HAD
HAPPENED TO HER

CHARLEY'S LARGE FOUR-SQUARE RESIDENCE BLAZED IN ALL directions as Myra, one rainy evening, turned her sedan into his driveway.

The consensus was that Charley kept his home ablaze because Polly, in her time, had been one to tweak out lights on every possible occasion.

"Darned if I wouldn't as soon live in a Christmas tree," commented John Henry.

"I'll be back to pick you up here about nine-fifteen."

"Don't see why I have to be farmed out over here every Friday when you go to your mother's. I'd rather stay home and look at television. There's wrestling tonight."

Myra could not explain that her reluctance to leave him to himself these Friday evenings was because it might conceivably bring home to him that there he sat alone, because his mother-in-law was so remote from him in way of life and language that visits to her home could only emphasize that never the twain could meet.

The visits and the questions they evoked from John Henry were sufficiently painful on the annual birthday occasions. "Do all Jewish old ladies keep their purses in their petticoat pockets so that they have to lift their skirts to even pay the butcher boy? Is it the Jewish way for men to sit in the house with their hats on?" John Henry put these questions uncritically. He asked to know.

Throughout the years of her marriage Myra parked her car, these Friday evenings, a block away from the house. Her mother did not ride from *Shabbes* Eve to *Shabbes* sundown. She knew of course that Myra did, and had, even when she lived at home. But somehow now that her mother was so alone, she did not want to drive up to the door after sundown.

For eighteen years these homecomings had been a matter of routine duty. But now, suddenly—something had happened to her. Was she growing old and returning to the way of life of her childhood? That happened. Old people on their deathbeds were often known to revert to ways of thought and living that had long since been put into the discard. She had read of agnostics returning on the deathbeds to the faith of their childhood. Not that she ever belied her religion, not observing it to be sure, but never denying it.

Her mother, sharp-eyed as a sparrow, was seated in her usual black beside the window, the ritual candles not yet lighted, her habitual guest and neighbor, old Mr. Topel, newly widowered, bent with the weight of his grief, seated beside her.

Despite his pension and small nest egg from the years as

presser in a dress factory, shades of the nursing home now hung over Topel. Neighbors took turns helping to keep his little home cleaned. These same good people also alternated at inviting the childless widower for meals. He seemed to find special solace at Mrs. Goldonsky's, and she gladly welcomed him to her board. Every so often Myra brought him a bottle of schnapps, which he marked with a pencil after each drink.

He clung to Mrs. Goldonsky, who had also known his wife over the years. In fact his almost constant presence gave her little privacy. But when Myra so much as broached this, her mother became matriarchal.

"You should be ashamed, Myra. It is a saying in Polish that turn away a friend and you will live yourself to be turned away by a friend. The *goyim* do not hold together like us, who have been chased through the centuries."

Seated in the chiaroscuro twilight, it struck Myra that both her aged mother and Mr. Topel might have walked out of a scene in the Old Testament.

The candles already lighted knitted shadows over the dinner table, which was spread and waiting. The twisted loaf of bread, or *challah*, covered with its prayer cloth, the prayer book and skullcap beside Topel's plate, were in place, the smells standing, as if also waiting. Gefüllte fish, which had taken Mrs. Goldonsky the greater part of a day to prepare, clear soup with finely cut noodles, chicken that had been boiled to yield that soup, prunes and carrots mixed into a sweet-potato mash, or *tzimmes*, warmed on the kitchen stove.

"I'll serve up in a few minutes."

"Where is Meena, Mama?"

"I'm glad when she goes home for *Shabbes*. If I had my way she should stay there the rest of the days in the week, that's how much I need a hired maid."

"Please, Mama, don't start with her or she'll leave. That will be the sixth or seventh this year."

"I start with her? It's she who starts with me."

"Whoever, Mama, I am afraid the next time it will have to be a professional companion. John Henry and I won't have you alone."

Topel, who seldom contributed to these discussions, nodded approval.

"But what has a girl to do here, Myra? Everything works by itself. A dishwasher does the dishes. The pressure cooker that came last week makes a pot roast in an hour that I like better should simmer half a day. And the mixer you sent yesterday is a fine present, I appreciate it, but it mixes me up more than it does the vegetable juices."

"Are you drinking your juices regularly, Mama?"

"I wish you would leave me alone with the newfangled notions. I have lived this long without them. So has Topel. Carrot and celery juice? Am I a rabbit? How a girl used to the food you were raised on can get used to such *goy* mishmash!"

But was she used to it? Yes, of course. Yet how, sitting here in this candlelit room with the old man and her strong-featured mother, could she be experiencing this sense of belonging?

Even beneath the crayon stares of those horrible wall portraits which had been the bane of her childhood, she felt secure here. John Henry had inquired, "Are those portraits

97

of your relatives?" She recalled with shame that she had replied with shame.

"I suppose so. I never knew them."

"Which is your father?"

"The second one."

She was knowing them all with her blood, as she sat there waiting for Friday-evening prayers to begin.

On went her mother, whose aged voice had become high and shrill as a parrot's.

"Topel, my daughter kills me with kindness. How can I make her see a servant girl in the house—and such a *schlomp* in the bargain—is in my way?"

"Mama, suppose you needed someone in the night?"

"Her neighbors," interposed Topel. "I'm one."

Mrs. Goldonsky suddenly lifted her skirt and plunged her hand into her petticoat pocket. "I got a letter from your Aunt Hanka in Israel. She's alone now since her boy was killed in the war. Maybe I should go to her there."

Topel stirred uneasily.

"Israel, Mama?"

"Your papa and I said there should be a place in the world which our people could call home. Hanka goes on to say in her letter that even if she was born in Warsaw, it was not until the day she set foot in Israel that she knew what home meant."

It occurred to Myra that this shabby little house on School Street was her homeland. That old upright piano in the corner, which her mother had managed to haggle in their leanest years from a secondhand dealer for sixty dollars, represented homeland. Likewise her own photograph in white dress, diploma in hand, taken upon the occasion of her graduation, with honors, from the Kunkel Music School. A samovar shining darkly in a corner. A scene that might have been painted by Josef Israels.

"Maybe it is better I should end my days with Hanka in the land where our people lived two thousand years ago. Besides, I would not be such a burden to you."

"Mrs. Goldonsky, you shouldn't say such things!"

"Topel is right, Mama. You know how both John Henry and I have tried to prevail upon you to come and live with us."

In a house where I have never yet set foot, was what Mrs. Goldonsky did not utter aloud. Time and time again she had wanted to accept the invitations to meals out of deference to the liberality of her—she could not quite bring herself to say "son-in-law"—out of deference to the liberality of Myra's husband.

But this marriage, with all its affluence and security for both Myra and herself, was actually a morsel of Dead Sea fruit that stuck in her throat and would not go down. She thanked God, chastizing herself for blasphemy the while, and wondered if it were blasphemy, that Myra had no children who would have been little mongrels, half *goy*. Go live in that house!

Mrs. Goldonsky's prejudices were suppurating wounds that would not heal. Her people were covered with them, and those who walked away from the sight of their wounds repudiated their race.

This daughter, dear as she was, and her husband, generous as he was, were actually little more than strangers. Their faces as she lay wakeful in the dark of her nights floated around her, lily pads on gloomy waters, remote, alien.

Myra, child of her body, gone in an absence stranger than the grave, because she was within touch, yet, to Mrs. Goldonsky's fathomless grief, gone.

Chapter 18

MR. PIRNER MAKES
A CLICKING SOUND
WITH HIS TONGUE

THE REVEREND POLKINHORNE AND HIS MOTHER WERE STILL housed in the handsome residence of T. H. Pirner, president of the Pirner Pharmaceutical Company and of the Rock Church congregation.

Meanwhile, as voted by the Board of Governors, the rectory was being enlarged by the addition of a four-room wing.

Personally Reverend Polkinhorne would have preferred to leave it untouched. The size seemed adequate, even in the face of future eventualities, and the red-brick Victorian structure, ivy-grown, its mullioned windows reaching to the floor, woodwork and indoor shutters black walnut, seemed to retreat quietly from a more harried and hurried era.

But the changes carried obvious implications, not to be ignored.

In fact, host Pirner, a gale of a man in his seventies, had come out with it in so many words, when he had assigned the Polkinhornes to a handsome three-room suite in the wing of his home that overlooked a fine sweep of country.

"We're trying to make you permanent here, Pastor. If you like us as much as we like you, that's the way it's going to be. Don't mind telling you that the specifications for the new wing on the rectory include a room that can be converted to a nursery in a jiffy when needed."

Mr. Pirner looked at Mrs. Polkinhorne and made a clicking sound with his tongue. She smiled and nodded.

That night, their first in the temporary quarters, the Reverend and his mother were seated before a great silver bowl of fruit that the maid who had turned back their beds had deposited on their living-room table, sharing an apple.

Regarding him, awareness moved to the front of his mother's mind that she seldom allowed there.

Unction coated her dear pastor-son, not only his pulpit manner, but he spoke in that same vein to his parishioners in their homes, his mother in hers, to himself inwardly.

Men were not at ease in Phillip's company, she knew that. But it seemed he no longer struggled to break through this invisible barrier by way of the slap on the back, the occasional drink, the lusty word. No matter what, pastor still stuck out all over him.

In women, on the contrary, his long white face, his long white hands, his light blue eyes that could fill with black, conjured seemingly unrelated thoughts. A husband with wide thick hands who cracked his knuckles. A fiancé with a bullish neck and football shoulders.

In women the Reverend inspired frustration. But not in his mother. He was her favorite, but she wished that like his brothers, Phillip had hair on his chest and on his voice.

"Our good host couldn't have been much plainer, could he, son?"

Apparently bent on peeling the apple in an unbroken strip, the Reverend continued to pare carefully.

"What do you mean, Mother?"

"Now, now, son, as if you don't know."

He regarded her with a fond, slow smile. "I can guess."

"Don't you agree with what Mr. Pirner meant?"

"I suppose a pastor worth his flock should be married."

"No, as much as I want it for your happiness, it mustn't be just because it is expected of you."

"I want it too, Mother," he said, the gravity back in his face, "I want it very much. I don't aim to be the only one of us brothers not to endow you with grandchildren. I hope to give you several."

She reached for his hand and held it. "How soon, Phillip?"

"I have tried to settle it in my mind during your visit. But there is only a week left."

"It would have been wonderful. But one does not settle these matters unless he is very very sure."

"It isn't that I am looking for another flaming romance, rather something right and quiet."

"And filled with God, as you are, son."

"You mean as filled with God as I yearn to be, Mother."

Her soft face indicated everything she felt.

"No man is really worthy of a good woman."

"That is what I ask for you, Phillip. A good woman through and through. I only wish your father was well enough for me to feel sufficiently easy in my mind to stay longer. Inner beauty shines through even a plain girl."

He knew to whom she referred.

"You have both, Mother. Beauty of body as well as soul."

"Hush your nonsense, Phillip."

"Come out with what is on your mind, Mother, or should I say with who is on your mind?"

"Your brothers all made their own choices without interference from your father or me, and they have been wise ones. Yours will be too, even though a man of the cloth needs a very special kind of wife."

"You like Clarabelle Sprague!"

"I don't want to influence you, Phillip, unless your own feelings also dictate. But in my humble judgment, there is a girl who would further your every interest. A pure, quiet girl in this age of so much boldness in young people—smoking, drinking, and all that goes with it."

"Blossom Eberhardt smokes, Mother."

"I know that, son. All my daughters-in-law smoke too, except Jean. I don't mean to seem stuffy, but a man of the cloth has so many special things to consider."

"I know pastors' wives who smoke, Mother, and even take an occasional cocktail."

"Of course, if you find greater values in Blossom . . ."

"You are being grand in all this, Mother."

"Everything that is good for you is the great wish of your father and me. Your brothers have blessed us with grandchildren—our lives will not be rounded until——"

"Mother, you make me want to read something especially lovely for our good night. What shall it be?" He crossed to his portfolio and withdrew a Bible.

"Read the Twenty-third Psalm, son, slowly . . ."

Chapter 19

I AM WHAT I AM

CHARLEY HAD REASON TO DISLIKE THE HIGH WINDS which could wrap themselves around his big home. The sounds reminded him of certain high laughter he had such bitter cause to remember. Polly's.

He wished to heaven, one clear December night of such racket, that things would stop rattling. The bottle of capsules and the water carafe on his night table. The windowpanes. A man could not sleep for din. Polly's kind.

But din was not the sole reason he tossed on his double bed. Windy nights were disturbing, but not sufficiently so, he reasoned, to account for the total wakefulness plaguing him these several weeks. Normally a sound sleeper, he was increasingly prone nowadays to lie wide-eyed in the darkness. What the dickens . . . ?

But Charley must have sensed, subconsciously at least, what-the-dickens. Now that he was free he wanted a woman to share the big wide bed with him, but not furtively. He wanted a wife. He wanted Virgie.

The beating of that name inside his head as he tossed or walked the floor through these long slow nights, left him unrested.

A man of his position must face up to the realities of introducing a Virgie into it. Night after night Charley faced up to it. The longer he cogitated, the greater his indecision. Yet what had he to lose? But in spite of himself, his grown children, toward whom he no longer acknowledged responsibility, clogged his thinking.

It was during this period of soul-searching indecision and harassment that the idea of the Sprague Memorial Hospital took shape in his mind and conscience.

Now was a time to entrench himself still more solidly into his community!

High tax bracket had frozen much of his incentive to amass further wealth to add to his immense holdings. By now, practically out from under most of them, except in the capacity of chairman of various boards, new leisures were threatening him from many sides. His secret fear of a recurring vascular pain, despite unanimity among doctors that the heart was not involved in these twinges, also played its part in his decisions to lighten the load. His daughter Claudia, who seemed lost, temporarily at least, in the maze of her own tangled life, had her own absorbing concerns. Brock, whom he had exposed to one executive opportunity after another, was proving himself capable of little more than holding down a managerial position, contrived at that, in one of the smaller holding companies.

At first there had been stormy scenes between the two of

them. Charley's immense temper, which years back, with the long-time help of a psychologist, he had learned to control, was again erupting through his acquired controls.

But recurring twinges around the region of his heart proved effective discipline. Charley now began to attempt the reasoning processes he had learned during his months under psychotherapy. Processes conceivably identified with secret drinking or dark vice might be at work in Brock. He decided to watch the course of events as they related to this boy upon whom he privately doted. To stand by, even humor.

Immersed in his alonenesses, his pleasures were few. Travel? He did not want to find himself stricken while away from home with the doggone twinges. Golf, cards, quail shoots did not fill a life.

It was out of these last realizations, together with an uneasy compulsion to atone to Polly's memory for what promised to be the detour in his life so irresistibly suggested by Virgie, that the idea for the memorial began to enlarge.

First it came in the form of a huge million-dollar gift to the city of St. Louis. Sprague Park? Sprague Auditorium? Sprague Stadium? He had earned the right to keep the name alive. Then the flash! Sprague Memorial Hospital for the Treatment of Mental Diseases.

Excitement flooded him. He could scarcely wait for daylight, and hours before dawn was down in the kitchen, preparing coffee. Whatever I may do with the rest of my life, I will have created a monument in her memory.

This is it. A memorial to Polly. I still remain a rich man, to say nothing of tax exemptions, and I'll be honoring her.

Excitement overran him. Waiting for dawn, he wandered from room to room, turning on more and more lights. In what he called his gun room, which was little more than an alcove, partitioned off from the billiard room by a screen, he whiled away the time by removing his collection of firearms one by one from the racks and replacing them, examining a pair of hip boots for possible leaks, staring at a row of framed prints of quail.

A few hours before dawn he picked up a telephone receiver, dialed, laid it back in its cradle without waiting for response, re-examined shotguns, picked up a volume entitled *Quail, Their Habits and Habitats*, replaced it, returned to the telephone, dialed once more.

"Hello, Virgie? It's Charley. Did I wake you? . . . Can't sleep. Anything in the way of my coming along for a while? . . . No, nothing is wrong. Just thinking of you. . . . Wait half an hour?" He did not inquire why. "I'll be along."

His mind was galloping. He had found the solution. A memorial. And now he could not wait.

It was toward five o'clock when Virgie opened the door to him.

Tall, still fairly slender except for the spread around her middle and the intimation of a second chin, her blondness only slightly tarnished, she wore with artlessness a ruffled, old-fashioned nightgown beneath a pink negligee thrown over her shoulders, her hair in a braid down her back.

"What's eating you, honey?" she asked without surprise, helping him strip off his coat and leading him to a chair which had an adjustable back.

"You," he replied without preamble, drawing her down onto his lap and pressing a kiss against her neck. "You, you, you," he added, pressing three more.

She lay softly against him. "You in love with me, honey?"

"Can't sleep with being it."

"I'm glad," she said dreamily. "I have to be loved. But more than that, you want to know something, Charley, I have to love more than I'm loved?"

"There never was a woman with so much to give."

"Don't say that, Charley. I'm not what you're used to."

"What has that to do with it?"

"Nothing, I guess, if you don't think it has."

"Don't give a damn."

"Then love me, Charley. That's all I need, to be loved and to love."

Her eyes were so blue, and in them stood enshrined all her tenderness and compassion. He reached up and tweaked out the light, drowning them into darkness.

When daylight finally showed between the drawn curtains he was repeating to her, "Marry me, Virgie." And she was repeating to him, "But you don't know me well enough."

"The sum total of what I need to know is that I want to marry you."

"I—can't believe it! You've never asked me about it, but I've been around, Charley."

"Can't help it."

"Yes, you can."

"How?"

"By getting me out of your hair."

"I don't want you out."

"I've been married, Charley, I've told you that much, or haven't I?"

"Are you now?"

"Not after a manner of speaking."

"What do you mean, 'not after a manner of speaking'?"

"Just that. Grant's—father died just before he was born. I was sixteen."

"I see."

"My second husband, Matt, went off one day three years after we were married. Disappeared, it will be five years ago come September."

"A fellow could actually walk out on somebody like you!"

"It was drink with him too, Charley. Longshoremen work hard and drink hard. Those were tough years. Matt not himself two-thirds of the time. After a way of thinking, God was good to me the day he walked out of my life. But God hit me hardest when my boy was mustered out of the Navy and mustered himself out of my life."

"You've had more than your share, girl."

"I've cried enough at night to bring him home on an ocean of tears."

"How do you manage financially, or is it a nerve to ask?"

"Who's got a better right, Charley?"

"If you put it that way, nobody, honey!"

"I can't force you to take what I'm going to say for what it is, word for word true, but so help me, it is."

"I'll take it for true, unsaid, if that's the way you'd like it."

"There was a fellow, Charley—a man, lived in my mother's boarding house as long as I can remember. He was three times my age—Charley Browne, a widower. He was an insurance agent, a retired one, toward the end. A saving man, one to have a nest egg."

"Charley Browne. Charley after Charley in your life."

"Only one, I'd say," she said, placing her palm against his cheek. "Well, anyway, the same year my mother had

passed on and I was waitressing, Charley Browne—well, he—
Charley dies too and—well he——"

"Don't bother to tell me any more, Virgie, so I can prove
I believe it without even hearing it."

"God love you! But anyway, Browne dies and leaves me
six thousand dollars' life insurance and cash on hand amount-
ing to about twenty-eight hundred."

"I'll be darned!"

"I'm not a brain trust in finances, honey, but I've been
able to make out on it, helping downstairs in Rotcheks'
Grocery Store five mornings a week when he can use me,
and not always living up my interest money at that. I make
out."

He laid kisses against the back of her hand. "My poor
Virgie. My dear, dear Virgie."

"I'm not poor Virgie, but I want to be dear Virgie."

"I almost wish you were the crying kind, so you would
do it on my shoulder—what with Grant—and all."

"Grant is only human, Charley. When a man marries
beyond what he is born to, he either takes the bull by the
horns and says, 'This is the way it is; you may as well know
my real background,' or he doesn't. Well, Grant didn't."

"I'll say."

"It was no crime, only maybe a little weakness. His father-
in-law is English, and I understand they care about class.
Grant always had it. Although, goodness knows, he didn't
get it from me or his father. I never would have intruded
in his life; he should have known that."

She did not cry, but was becoming scarcely audible
through a tightening throat.

With a sudden lift in tone and manner, he drew her by

the shoulders face to face with him. "Now let's you and me talk about you and me! The time has come for Virgie and Charley to be important to ourselves and not look back."

"Listen, Charley, you've got position, you've got kids. Suppose Matt should ever show up?"

"You let me worry about everything. As for my children, they are taken care of and there is more ahead for each of them."

"There are your brothers."

"So what? John Henry is almost as well-heeled as I am, and I don't owe my brother Ed one damned thing. Time and time again I've gone out of my way to let him in on big deals, the same as I did for John Henry. But Ed and his entire family have ideas of their own. His children don't want any of my kids, and mine want none of them. I can't help there, and I've stopped trying."

"Are you sure you can't, Charley? You remember the saying, 'Peace, it's wonderful.'"

"I don't know much about that, but I'm taking care of the memory of my wife. A memorial to her that will set this town back on its heels. I did my part while she was aboveground, and now that she is under, I'm entitled to what's left of my life!" he exploded and ground more kisses against her. "I want to marry you."

"Pinch me, Charley, so I'll know it's true."

He pinched her cheek between thumb and forefinger. "There never was so much woman in one woman."

"Pinch me again, Charley. This wonderfulness can't be true."

This time, because she was a lusty woman and could give

it back, he dared to be vulgar, and gave it to her on the posterior, and she laughed and gave it vulgarly back.

"God, I love a woman who is herself. I've never been my-self before. I'm still laughing over that salt-pork story you told the other night. We'll each begin making up for lost time, won't we, Virgie?"

"You said it, honey."

"When? I'd marry you tomorrow, if I had my way."

"But, Charley, according to law——"

"My lawyers will find a way."

"Don't you think I've checked on it already? There's a friend of mine who comes here who in his good days was a district attorney in Richmond, Virginia. He claims that in Missouri the law says one year—that is, if things can be proved—is considered desertion and seven years for some additional red tape. I've forgotten what. But any way you look at it, there is a long rigmarole and the chance that Matt may show up again."

"How long did you say it was since you've had word of him?"

"Chuck Friedlander, a friend of his, ran into him about a year ago in Manila. He sent me a message he was coming back. So you see, Charley, what a mess for you this all might mean. Matt's rough. Big rough."

"So am I, baby, if need be."

"Besides, Charley, it's wonderful that you never pry, but there are more things you ought to know about me."

"I know wonderful things about you without being told."

"I guess you've noticed that I'm not always as—well, I guess you'd call it discreet—as I should be."

"Have I said so?"

"There was someone here when you telephoned tonight."

He rose, walked to the window, and stood staring through it.

"I'm just that way, Charley," she said, rising too, but not following. "The someone, when he gets into one of the depressions he's been subject to since Guadalcanal, comes to me. I guess I'm a pushover."

"What do you mean—a—pushover?" he asked with his back still turned.

"Just what I say. One of those do-gooders who thinks they're needed. Do you get it?"

"I guess I do."

"There's nothing in it for me. I've enough to live on if I cut corners, but I am what I am, Charley."

He stood.

"It's the first time a man like you has ever been around, much less asking what you're asking me. I could cry, if I wasn't ashamed to. I've always been ashamed to cry. I guess that's why I laugh so much."

She covered her face, and the long silence lengthened.

Finally he turned, sat her down on the divan, and drew up a straight chair. "I've got to have you Virgie, no matter how. I know that now."

"You're offering me heaven."

"I want to live with you, lay with you, be with you for the rest of my life, may it be a long one. I want to hurt you, that's how much I love you."

"Then hurt me."

"God forgive me, Virgie, I had a good wife, but I am born tonight, loving for the first time. Be good to only me, Virgie. I'm your man now."

"You're my man," she repeated, holding his cheeks in the vise of her hands and boring into his eyes with hers.

"I'll see my lawyer. There must be a way for us to get married. Immediately. My God, the man has disappeared! What are you supposed to do? Wait your life away? I'll be damned if you will."

"Be blessed instead, Charley. We can be married this minute!"

"Not soon enough."

"We can speak our marriage vows right here—now, before God. The Bible doesn't say they must be administered by a clergyman or a magistrate. Even a sea captain can do it. Who will know the difference if we speak our marriage vows between us?"

"The world, Virgie."

"Why? We eloped to a far-off city. We'll be away for a few days. Who is going to demand our certificate?"

"But, Virgie, the woman, especially in this situation, has a right to be protected by law."

"You are my law. Should Matt ever show up—and I'm not ashamed to say, 'Please God he won't'—we will have broken no laws because in the eyes of the law we will not be married."

He walked once more over to the window and slashed back the curtains so that the brass rings grated along the rod and the early sun moved in.

She shoved a small table into its brightness, placed a vase of artificial pink roses from the mantel in the center, and extracted a small worn Bible from under the cushion of a chair.

"Come, Charley."

They stood side by side, facing the light.

"Say: 'I take thee, Virginia Ellen, to be my lawful wife.'"

"I take thee, Virginia Ellen, for my wedded wife."

"I take thee, Charley, to be my wedded husband, to love, honor, and obey."

"Until death do us part, darling."

"Until death do us part, my darling."

Chapter 20

A STRANGELY
PEREMPTORY CALL

Brock was surprised at himself. But for several weeks he had been awakening in his room at the Metropolis Club with the same thought. He was seriously contemplating going back home to live.

For years he had occupied one of the club rooms. There were only about ten in all, allocated to "permanent guests."

He had liked the way of life, the pleasant accessories available. Gymnasium, swimming pool, indoor tennis and handball, barbershop, first-rate dining room, leather-smelling lounges, cards, newspapers, magazines, bar.

Here a man could follow his own impulses for privacy or companionship. Occasionally Brock gave small dinner parties in the handsomely appointed dining room, either for men friends or, on ladies' nights, for mixed groups.

The headwaiter, a white-haired Negro who had occupied this position for two decades, needed no instruction as to his preferences in menu, wine, flowers. In addition, his pleasant room was within five minutes' walking distance of his office in the Missouri Building.

He had postponed speaking to his father about his growing intention of returning to West Grove, not certain that mood would last. But there it was each morning, the same desire, only larger than it had been the day before.

Of this much he felt certain: his old man would welcome him. Not that the death of his mother, who had been out of the home since his childhood, had altered his father's aloneness, but somehow, since her passing, the picture of the solitary figure in that twenty-two-room "museum piece" of a house, as he and his sister had long since tagged it, lived with Brock.

And there was something more. Two monkeys rode Brock's back, though he had actually succeeded in throwing off one. It had been off now for a length of time sufficient to restore his confidence, his body, his soul.

True, there were still moments when the burning and craving rose to plague him, but they had diminished in frequency and intensity almost to the vanishing point. By the picking up of a telephone receiver he could summon aid to help to fight the fight.

He had somehow found the wisdom to take himself in hand early in the history of his cravings by joining the Friends in Need.

Fairly early, he began to understand the hazards of the solitary drinker, especially when he lay in a half stupor in his bed while the morning climbed toward noon and his small office force began to suspect.

A chance remark overheard in an elevator had led him to Friends in Need, a national organization dedicated to aid the alcohol addict in the throat-and-soul-searing hoist out of his abyss.

The twelve laws of the organization, pasted inside his wallet, were strong rope under his armpits during the early stages of the torturous process. When the burn began to move up through his body into his throat there was also the telephone, and the immediate response of a fighter in the same fight rushing to him.

It was six months now since Brock had tilted a bottle, ten weeks since he had sent out a call for help. His big test had come the night he lay wakeful, craving, but with the bottle of liquor uncorked on the table beside him.

Actually this monkey on his back was there because of a previous terrible concern.

Ever since his discharge from the Army, a conviction that his sanity was slipping would come periodically to roost with him.

In the midst of a business conference he would feel his mind suddenly lock, shutting him out from where he was or from what he was doing, the supreme effort of pushing his way back causing him to break into a sweat, occasionally noticeable. The night sweats were the worst. As if exploding awake, he would find himself on his feet, fighting for orientation. Where am I? Who am I? My name, for God's sake, my name! Sometimes switching on a light would bring him back. It was mollifying to attribute these bouts with terror to nightmare. But again there were times when, riveted to the bed, he suffered the night through, separated from himself, filled with a turmoil of fear of another presence in the room. His slightest movement might mean death. Through eyelids he kept resolutely closed, sometimes there was a face peering. His mother's.

Madness lay this way. His mother's madness?

He had once seen his father go off into a fit of uncontrollable blaspheming rage, a kind of strangulation that seemed to verge on apoplexy, because a gardener had taken a rifle from its rack in the gun room and accurately shot roses off a bush.

No one who viewed that scene, including the gardener and two servants who left shortly after, was ever to forget it. Stark terribleness.

He had not even confided in his sister, with whom he frequently swapped confidences regarding their "old man." Claudia's marriage shortly after Brock's divorce had changed that relationship.

But withal, there managed to survive between Brock and his father a rooted affection which sprouted in barren circumstances, a bit of green struggling through a crack in the asphalt.

There was something immensely lonely, fastidiously private and uncomplaining about his old man. Something pretty grand about the seemingly relaxed ease with which he had made himself and John Henry rich men. Claudia attributed much of it to what she termed her father's "*in* with luck." To be sure, the old man, like a bird dog on the follow, seemed to find the scent to success. Many was the project he let lie and, more often than not, wisely. No doubt about it, the old gentleman had something!

Nevertheless, awareness of his father's capacity for mental explosion was also part of Brock's tormenting fears of what he might be inheriting from his parents.

Time after time he went to the brink of a decision to consult a general practitioner or a psychiatrist, but, dominated by fear of what he might learn, drew back.

In a locked desk drawer was an item headed "Various Types of Dementia Praecox," which he had clipped from a newspaper medical column.

Sometimes in the watches of a bad night he removed the item for rereading, although he knew its contents.

Catatonic type: Peculiarities of conduct with phases of stupor or sex excitement . . .

Paranoiac type: Characterized by prominences of delusions, persecution, or grandeur. . . .

Hebephrenic type: These show tendency to silliness, peculiar often bizarre ideas, neologisms or coining of meaningless words, hallucinations.

None of these took precise account of his kind of torments, but paranoic-hebephrenic came closest. Delusions. Hallucinations. Why and what about the sudden swoop of terror in the pit of his stomach? The sweats induced by the faces that swam in his darkness? The lapses when he found himself standing off from himself and staring at himself?

Another reference in the same article caused his tongue to go dry. "From the point of view of the hereditability of a predisposition to develop a disease, it is important to get an accurate statement of the patient's family history. The personal history should contain detailed information concerning the life and habits of the parents, their emotional adjustments . . ."

Every so often the attacks would disappear for weeks on end, the hours at his office and his nights uninterrupted by chimeric visitations. It seemed to him that these intervals were widening. He took to marking the length of them on his calendar. His spirits lifted.

And now, unaccountably, so it seemed to him, he was wanting a life with his old man.

But that too added to his bother. What did his sudden gyration indicate? Since his broken marriage, he had remained out of the home by preference. Meanwhile his old man had long since ceased to storm over his inadequacies, and worse, in the various Sprague enterprises.

In addition, the old man had softened appreciably in these years since a psychologist had succeeded in taming the outbursts of temper which in Brock's childhood had made home life explosive.

Brock was prayerful that some of his father's stamina in conquering his tiger of a temper was now manifesting itself in him. The thought gave him hope and the desire to resume life at home.

He now felt ready to take up management of the affairs that for years had forced his father to call in a so-called assistant manager to cover up his son's impotence.

He needed a revealing talk with his father. But he learned from his Uncle John Henry that Charley was suddenly off on a ten-day business trip, giving no details.

Evidently he was spending some "lettuce" on the old house too, because when Brock drove past it during those ten days of his absence, two furniture vans were unloading before the door and men were at work on the lawns.

They were saying that Charley, after all the years of conformity to his tragedy, was "stepping it up." Good for him! Brock hoped the turn of affairs was bringing his old man, as well as the old house, rejuvenation.

It was while he was thus marking time that a long-distance telephone call from his father came through from Colorado.

I want you and your sister to be at the house day after tomorrow. About eight in the evening. Important.

A strangely peremptory order, thought Brock as he hung up and dialed a call to Claudia.

Chapter 21

DO US SOMETHING

CHARLEY HAD SO MANAGED IT THAT HIS RETURN WITH Virgie from points west occurred twenty-four hours in advance of his announced arrival.

It seemed expedient to spend that time in Virgie's half-dismantled apartment, where the "Vacancy" sign was already plastered against the window.

"Do you know how many years I've lived in this flat, Charley? Twenty-two."

"And the next from-now-to-eternity years will be spent with me on Roxbury Road, West Grove."

She sat on his knee in the half-stripped room, looking a little slimmer and younger in a navy-blue skirt and red blouse with fluted ruffles cascading down its front, her light hair drawn back into a curly chignon.

"Pretty girl," he said, as if contemplating her for the first time.

"Try never to see me as I am, honey. Tarnished Tillie."

"But I can't get used to you in daytime togs. Can't wait to settle down with you at home and get you back into those nightgowns or whatever it is you wear in the house."

"Negligees."

"Well, whatever, they excite me."

"Charley," she said, fingering his tie as she talked, "I hate to wish time away, but if only we were a week older."

"Quit stewing. We don't owe anybody anything. Tomorrow we're going home. Our home, you hear!"

"Who will be in the house when we get there?"

"Want me to go all over that again? All right. Exactly nobody. That's why I selected Sunday. The housegirl is out and our old cook, whom I've pensioned now, only comes in at about four to fix dinner. You can change all that to suit yourself."

"Then your—son—and daughter won't arrive until evening?"

"Yes, I told him to show up with his sister tomorrow night about eight."

"Honey, aren't you nervous? It will be a bombshell for them."

"I keep telling you, baby, I don't owe anybody one word of explanation. Neither do you. In fact, the less we both try to explain, the better. We're mister and missus. Do us something."

"Charley, why does it have to be as soon as tomorrow night—our first day—home?"

"Because you are making such a production of it I want it over so you will stop worrying. I'm not saying it's easy to go through, but it's been done a million times before and will be done a million times after us."

"But let's face it, Charley. I am what I am, and they are what they are."

"And what you are is what I want and what I've got," he said, crushing her to him.

"Why don't we have it all over at once, Charley, with the rest of your family?"

"I feel I kind of owe it to my kids to let them be the first. Maybe they aren't all I had hoped they would be, but they'll be smart enough to realize in pretty quick order that I have brought home a prize package. They'll love you."

"And I'll love them."

"They have practically had no mother. If the truth be known, neither have they had a father. It has worried the daylights out of me, but I just didn't seem to have the talent for it."

"My poor darling."

"You mean your lucky darling."

"Oh, Charley, I just can't wait to begin to be the comfort that you need me to be."

"We need each other, Virgie, and we've got each other."

Chapter 22

THEY CAN HAVE
THEIR ULCERS

ON SATURDAY AFTERNOONS, WHEN WINTER PRECLUDED
father-and-son visits to the baseball park, Ed and Anchutz
usually puttered in the basement or went ice skating.

Clara worriedly contended that the sport was too strenu-
ous for a man Ed's age, but both he and Anchutz rode down
this objection.

Ed was still remarkably good on the steel blades. This was
a matter of pride to Anchutz. His old man's skating was up
to the best of the fellows, including himself.

Ed's satisfaction over this compatibility with his son was
simultaneously offset by a certain unease.

The boy did not get out enough, had too few friends of
both sexes. To be sure, there was Fred Kirsch, with whom
Anchutz shared his pigeon hobby. Occasionally he chose a
girl from Henschen's to take to a dance, but by far the greater
part of his free time, Anchutz hung about the home. Clara

too liked him there, but not, as she put it, tied to her apron strings. Youth should be young!

"Anchutz," she urged, "why don't you have more young people come here or you go to them? What about those dances they have every two weeks at the Y.M.C.A.?"

"That's for fellows who want them. Why don't you ask Clarabelle the same thing? I don't see her gallivanting."

"Gallivanting isn't what I mean, and you know it. That's just the point I'm making. If you don't care to take one of those nice girls who work at Henschen's, it would not hurt you to escort your sister. A girl has to be asked before she can attend a dance. It's different with a young man."

"What girl wants to go out with her own brother?" He did not add aloud, And who wants to take his own sister!

"I don't say you should always take your sister. But I do think you might bring more young men to the house."

Anchutz replied off the stock shelf of his retorts to such remarks. "Mom, you know well and good a girl has to make her own boy friends. Fellows simply won't be dragged."

"They should welcome the opportunity to meet a fine girl."

"Sure they should, but suppose they don't? Unless she uses her come-hither on them—and you wouldn't want her to be one of those."

This in turn was the cue for one of Clara's stock retorts, a sigh.

One blustery Saturday afternoon down in the basement, where Ed and Anchutz were engaged in fashioning birdhouses to be installed, come spring, in trees behind the house, Ed stopped sawing away at a plank and as if following up Clara's observation of the previous day, remarked, "Come over here and sit on the bench, Anchutz; I want to talk to you."

Not given to sudden impulses, Ed was later unable to explain to himself how this one had come about. Just flooded over him all of a sudden. Likewise taken unawares, Anchutz laid down his chisel and followed his father.

"Son, let's you and me talk out what's on my mind."

"Sure, shoot."

"Has it ever occurred to you that if you don't watch it, you're going to be a dead ringer for your old man?"

"Well, that's all right with me."

"Son, has it ever occurred to you that from a certain point of view your old man has got himself nowhere in the world?"

"What's the big idea?"

"That's just my point. I never had big ideas. Not that I'm complaining or regretting for myself. On the contrary, I chose it this way. I'm the man who has always wanted contentment above all, and to my way of thinking, power breeds discontent. But I'm wondering if you have the same temperament or have only been molded by the way of life your mother and I prefer. I've been thinking a long time that I ought to bring this up with you, possibly warn you off."

"Off what?"

"Taking life the way your mother and I have. Satisfied with remaining small. I couldn't have lived this way with another type of woman. I thank God plenty for your mother. But times have changed. You are not likely to find a girl today like your mother was, and is."

"Who says I'm looking?"

"Not now, perhaps. But the day will come."

"Not necessarily."

"I've watched you down at the firm. You are a steady, reliable worker. So am I. The higher-ups like you, the way they like me. Trotters in harness. But meanwhile, fellow after fellow with no more ability, but more unrest, is going to pass you by, and someday will be your boss. I know; I'm under a half-dozen of them now."

"They can have their ulcers."

"They had mine and still have them, and I haven't a regret for what else they have and I haven't. But I wouldn't deserve to be your father if I didn't want for you better than I had myself. Maybe I shouldn't say *better*. I've had and am having a good life."

"I believe that, Dad. Then why isn't it good enough for me?"

"Fine, if you're geared for it, but this much you should bear in mind: it is a new and different world. Take your uncles——"

"You take them, Dad."

"Now don't dismiss them that way. The fact that I wouldn't change places with either of them, and still feel exactly the same as I did the day I decided not to go in with them, doesn't make it right."

"It does with me."

"I'm not so sure I did the best by your mother and you children."

"We are."

"I don't know much about your cousins Brock and Claudia."

"We know enough."

"You must bear in mind there was practically no mother there."

"Mom did her part trying to be one to them, but they would have no truck with us."

"They were no more to us than we were to them. Much of it was my fault, and maybe your mother's too, who took her cue from me. We didn't seem to want the same things, and the strangeness between us just happened. I've nothing against them. Charley gave me a fair break in the beginning. Not that I had anything against being a rich man, but a man with two kids doesn't stick his neck out on a gamble. I can't imagine your uncles' ever needing me, but if they should, your mother and I would be right there."

"What's all this leading up to?"

"Exactly what I said. Most fathers are complaining just the opposite these days, but I'm not sure a fellow should spend all his free time hobnobbing with his dad, eating lunch with him every day, when there should be young people in his life."

"Damn it, I like being with you."

"That's a fine thing for a father to hear."

"I like it here at home better than in anyone else's home. I like it down at the firm, no matter how unambitious it sounds. I don't mind being passed up by the ulcer set of fellows, no matter how fine it seems for them to neck-and-neck it to get ahead. I look at Uncle Charley and John Henry, and they are good guys, I guess; but—let me be my way, Dad, even if it happens to be your way. Huh?"

Ed placed his hand on top of his son's. For a period they sat in a kind of abashed silence.

"Huh, Dad?"

Presently they were back, hammering and sawing away at the birdhouses.

Chapter 23

CAN'T HELP
LOVING THAT MAN

In response to their father's peremptory demand, Claudia and Brock arrived at the house on Roxbury Road separately, but with surprising promptness. Before they could do much more than exchange surmises, Charley entered, shaved, groomed, and with the terrible cocksureness of the unsure.

"Well," he said, with a new offhand manner born of inner turmoil and rubbing his palms together as if he wanted them to spark, "well, well." His daughter pecked his cheek and sat herself on the arm of a gold brocade chair into which her brother sank.

"Out with it, Dad. Are we in the doghouse, and if so, why?"

"I was married a week ago today in Texas."

Dangling one foot, Claudia lighted a cigarette. From his brocade lair Brock growled a slow, "I'll be damned."

"Who is she?" inquired Claudia, her coolness not betraying that it was mustered up.

"And where is she?" interposed Brock.

Charley, pacing up and down, paused before them. "She is upstairs in—our room, waiting for me to bring her down."

"She being who or whom?"

"My wife, the former Mrs. Virgie—Virginia Scogan."

"Scogan?"

"Do we—know her, Dad?"

"You will in a few minutes."

"Why did you choose to do it like this, Dad? Is it your way of taking us into your confidence?" asked Claudia, with coolness sustained.

"Don't make Dad laugh," said Brock. "We're seldom around here long enough for him to take us into his confidence or anything else."

"Your brother said it for me, Claudia. I needed this empty house to become a home."

"Is there anything about the lady you think we should know, Dad?"

"You've both the right to know, and I want you to know. You're going to meet one of God's finest."

"Where does she——"

"Virgie was born here in St. Louis. As a young person she enjoyed none of your advantages, but she is sweet to the core, and I mean to the core. A widow when I met her."

"Congratulations!" exclaimed Brock, rising and throwing an arm across his father's shoulder. "If that's the way you feel about the lady, that's all to the good, no matter what. And I'll say she's got a good egg! But wouldn't it happen

133

just as I am about to invite myself back to live in the old family manse with you? Wouldn't it!"

"As I've always told you both, your rooms, your home, are still yours. Now same as ever."

"Two is company, Dad."

"Not when you know Virgie. She is the biggest little adjuster you'll meet in a lifetime."

"Where did you meet her?" pursued Claudia, cupping her chin in her hand and regarding her parent with slow, inquiring eyes. "And when?"

"I met Virgie . . . let me see," replied Charley with elaborate concentration. "Must be about a year or so ago one night when I was having dinner with Isaiah Cronin in a restaurant. Oh yes, and there is a son too, but he's been down in Australia since the war."

"Australia?"

"Lay off the cross-examination, Claudia."

"I think Dad would want us to be interested, Brock."

"If I felt you were," said Charley somewhat sadly, "it might not have happened this sudden way."

"I feel rotten about not knowing, Dad."

"Don't we both! But Brock and I are happy about it if you are. Where did you say you were married?"

"Dallas."

"Why?"

"Just not to have any commotion."

"Where has your wife been living, Dad?"

"In town."

"Where?"

"On Pine."

"Pine Boulevard?"

"No, Pine Street. Lived there for many years."

"Pine—Street, did you say?"

"I said Pine Street. You heard me."

"I see."

"For Pete's sake, Claudia, you act as if Pine Street is a leper colony."

"Brock, will you please let me ask my own questions in my own way."

"Your sister has the right, Brock. So have you."

"You don't owe us any explanations, Dad."

"I want to give them. I also want to say right here that in return for the happiness this wonderful woman is bringing to me, I am going to reverse the wedding business and celebrate my marriage by giving each of you a hundred-thousand-dollar insurance annuity. Of course the memorial to your mother that I told you about is also not mine alone, but in your names as well."

"I just don't know what to say, Dad," said Claudia, rising.

"I do. You're just swell, Dad. I wish to God I could say as much for us—I mean, for me."

"You've missed having a mother over the years. Virgie will be the first to appreciate that."

"When do we meet the lady?"

"Now. There's a magnum of champagne on ice, Claudia. And ginger ale or anything soft for you, Brock, if you want it."

"Heaven forbid that I should stay on it tonight of all nights. Your wedding celebration."

"Go easy, then."

"We'll have it in the dining room, where all the fixings are ready. I'll bring Virgie down."

In a powder-blue dress, frilled with lace, and again so at variance with her flowing house gowns that Charley regretted that she had changed, Virgie, pacing before a pier glass in a bedroom of damask-covered walls that dated back to Polly, was talking to herself.

Make them like me. Don't let me fail him. We're married before you, God. We couldn't be any more married.

Charley, entering, caught her around the waist from the rear. "What are you saying to you, my pretty?"

"That I love you, Charley, and that please, please God I'll make you happy and that we're married in the eyes of God."

"In the eyes of God," he repeated and led her down the stairs. He could feel her arm trembling and wondered if perhaps it might not be his own.

But the "ordeal" did not materialize. On the contrary, the talk ran with a fair amount of ease. Charley spoke the prologue. "Children, this is Virgie, and Virgie, these are the children, and God bless us all," he said and tilted the magnum of champagne at the dining table. Katy, who dated back to Polly, served the cold buffet supper and lifted with them the glass of champagne which Charley poured for her.

Thus the occasion, with its base of stresses and strain, passed in badinage, Brock and Charley batting it back and forth, their jocosities labored but leavening, most of the levity directed by Brock.

"Don't let my Dad get too familiar with you, Virgie. Everything he touches is supposed to turn to gold, and then we would have to melt you down."

Her heart swelled when he called her "Virgie." Charley too was moved by Brock's efforts to lighten the occasion. Claudia likewise made her attempts but realized that their heaviness was worse than the silence and subsided into it.

"Take a stand in the beginning," pursued Brock. "Don't let my Dad wake you every morning before dawn because he can't sleep after five. Don't expect too much attention when he's broody over a new promotion project."

"What right have you two to gang up against me?" laughed Charley, bestowing one of his pinches upon Virgie's posterior, a familiarity which had gone unrebuked the first time and by now had become enjoyable habit.

"Charley, that isn't a nice thing to do—here."

Claudia widened her cool blue eyes. "Dad!"

"But a love pinch is all right in my book," quickly countered Virgie, and to spare Charley further embarrassment plopped herself across his lap, mussing his hair with five spread fingers.

"I just can't help loving that man!"

The phrase rushed over Claudia like a sandpapering job: "I just can't help loving that man!"

Why was this Virgie woman, with the broad streak of common in her, having her man, while she had let hers slip through her fingers, through her life, through her happiness? Why?

Yet, viewed in a certain way, this Virgie person was a godsend. Someone to care for her father as he aged, lifting the uneasy apprehension that someday an emergency, such as her father's illness or encroaching decrepitude, might necessitate her return to this big overgilded mausoleum of a house.

Virgie slid from the display of intimacy on Charley's lap in a state of flush and fluster. "You mustn't mind me," she said. "Someday when you know me better you'll realize I never had it so good—I mean, so good for loving. That is," she added hastily, "if you *want* to know me better——"

"Want to know how much I want to know you better?" exclaimed Brock, who, despite the watchful eye of his father, had tossed off three or four glasses of champagne. "I'm coming back home to live in my own third-floor kennel if it is all right with you and Dad."

"Is it, Virgie? I've always kept the children's quarters ready and waiting, in case——"

"Say, that will be fine, and mean a lot to your dad. And—and—won't you—be coming too——" For the life of her, she could not speak the name "Claudia" and bit it off the end of her remark.

"I have a house, you see," spoke Claudia, whose effort to thaw resulted in a kind of sweet iciness. Virgie regarded Claudia's prettiness and was silent, because something too subtle for her to fathom was in her way.

It was no occasion for reprisals, and Charley saw to it that there were none, even as he regarded Brock, whose eyes were becoming glassy.

"You slipped the trolley a bit tonight, son, and it's all right. But you are in no condition to drive to your club. Claudia, will you give your brother a lift in your car?" he said, and threw an arm along his son's shoulder, his mood sufficiently benign to embrace all.

Poor Brock. His eyes watered, drowning out his high resolve, but his handsome face managed to keep steady. "I'm moving in on you, Virgie," he repeated, and emboldened by his father, gave her a small whack where Charley had pinched.

In his sister's cream-colored convertible, which she drove with a sure hand, he kept repeating to himself, "Can't help liking that girl. Can't help loving that man."

"Can't help liking that girl."

Would she ever escape the rhythm of those mocking phrases! "Can't help liking that girl." "Can't help loving that man."

"You seem to have said that before, Brock."

He lapsed for a moment into his own thoughts.

Why try to help liking that gal? Weren't he and Claudia both gaining by this surprise move? Where had his father found her? He suspected where, from the rumors. A looker too, in her day.

"How did Dad ever fall for her, or she for him?"

"How did she ever? Don't make me laugh, Brock."

"There you go!"

"Do you know a girl in this town who would close her eyes to his bank account?"

"When Virgie said, 'I just can't help loving that man,' she wasn't giving lip service to a rich husband. She said it with her guts."

"I just can't help loving that man." Gaining momentum, the phrase began to whirl inside Claudia like a carrousel gone wild.

She was on her way home, but to an empty house, because crazily—God, how crazily!—she had let go from it a man whom, she was realizing too late, she could not help loving.

Chapter 24

ED WAS PARING
HIS TOENAILS

THE SPENCES, AS THEY WERE AFFECTIONATELY KNOWN, lived in a narrow brick house on Hightower Street. The three-storied interior belied its unsmiling front. It contained good mahogany, bright chintzes, polished brasses, and a pair of porcelain-frail Spences, both over seventy, one of them, Miss Ollie, chair-ridden.

Miss Ollie had been married, but sometimes it seemed to her she had only dreamed it. Fifty-one years back she had met a young physician, house doctor in a St. Louis hotel, on a Friday, married him the following Friday; and on the third Friday, crossing the street at Twelfth and Olive, he had been run down by a beer truck and killed outright.

The Misses Ollie and Janet lived in the house built by their grandfather. Miss Janet's schoolteacher pension and a tearoom, contrived out of their combined front and back parlors, contributed to the slender income left by their father.

Residents of West Grove, particularly members of the

Rock Church and the older citizenry in general, regarded patronage of the sisters' tearoom as a kind of obligation. The back parlor could be engaged for bridge or canasta parties, for the accommodation of ladies unequipped or undisposed to entertain at home. West Grove had also learned to beat a trail to Hightower Street for the excellently brewed tea or coffee, piping hot muffins, and homemade preserves which the sisters sold in prettified jars.

Since Miss Ollie had suffered a slight stroke, she remained for the greater part of the time upstairs in the pleasantly old-fashioned and well-cared-for sitting room beside a wire rack of growing potted plants which constituted her indoor garden. Mothers sent their children after school with small offerings for Miss Ollie, and the card-party guests almost invariably managed time out for a little visit with her.

The Ed Sprague residence stood back to back with the Spences'. By moving aside one of the boards of the dividing back fence, Clarabelle, squeezing through on her visits to Miss Ollie, usually with a napkin-covered plate in hand, could save a trip around the block.

Not infrequently she would spend part of her Saturday afternoons listening to the sometimes confused patter of a mind fading even more rapidly than the body it inhabited.

In winter, when the lights came on at early dusk, Clarabelle would peer across the yards, trying to determine by the outline of the figures whether there were guests up in Miss Ollie's room. Occasionally she could even discern their identities.

It was more considerate to choose a time when Miss Ollie was alone, thus spacing the diversion of visitors.

One lovely winter dusk that still held the glow of its sunset, Clarabelle felt certain she could detect the outline of Reverend Polkinhorne's head. A bit ashamed, she rummaged in a dresser drawer for her opera glasses.

She had not intended to visit Miss Ollie this particular afternoon, but, again ashamedly, she did over her hair, applied lipstick, and slid out of her office blouse into a sheer one with lace at the neck, and threw a coat across her shoulders, sleeves dangling.

The smells of her mother's dinner chicken, slowly simmering in its broth, wound upstairs, downstairs, and in my lady's chamber. With a little jar of it in hand, Clarabelle oozed through the fence, heartbeat high. After all, what was more natural than for her, on one of her visits to Miss Ollie, to encounter her pastor?

She was not the only one guilty of such subterfuge. It was common talk that girls from as far as St. Louis, Kirkwood, and Clayton were throwing themselves at the bachelor pastor's head, some of them from other denominations appearing at services—to say nothing of the obviousness of Blossom Eberhardt, who had chauffeured Reverend Polkinhorne the entire week that his car was up for repairs. And as if that were not sufficiently obvious, Blossom had subsequently made it a practice to place her services at the disposal of the Reverend's mother, driving her about to the many social functions in her honor during the hours he was occupied.

When Clarabelle burst in upon Miss Ollie and the Reverend, they greeted her with warmth.

"I hope I don't intrude."

"I would call her a welcome intruder, wouldn't you, Miss Ollie?" said Reverend Polkinhorne, rising to offer her his chair.

Poor Miss Ollie, whose mental processes moved slowly, commandeered her thinking with surprising focus.

"This girl, Reverend," she said in her gravel voice, "is God's gift to the world. Comes home from her work and finds time to come to me. Never empty-handed, never makes me feel it is a chore to come to see an old woman."

"But, Miss Ollie, it isn't a chore!"

"And she means it, Reverend. My sister and I always say Clarabelle Sprague was born to serve others. She's a good girl—none of the flighty drinking and smoking of the young people nowadays for her. She will be God's gift to some man."

Blushing up under her hair and down into her collar, Clarabelle turned to the Reverend. "You can see that Miss Ollie is a little bit partial."

"I agree with her all the way."

"I have lived a long time, Reverend, and seen girls grow up different from the way they were in my day, some good, some pretty bad, but here is one good girl."

In the beginning Clarabelle had been glad to be praised in the exciting presence of the pastor. But now that there was no stopping Miss Ollie, a dread rose in her that Miss Ollie might appear to be celebrating her virtues to an eligible man.

She rose in confusion. "I just ran over, dear, with some of my mother's chicken broth for your dinner; it's nice and hot. I'll see you again in a day or two."

The Reverend rose with her. "I'll be on my way too, Miss Ollie."

The old lady regarded them tremulously. "It's a pleasure to look upon a pair of young people like you. God bless you."

Out in the cold clear evening, a first star, Venus, shone large as a coin.

"I'll walk you home," he said. Instead of taking the short cut, they walked halfway around the block. Trembling with excitement, she lowered her voice to hold it in control, and when he hooked his hand into the crook of her arm she was afraid he might feel the tremble.

"A dear woman," he said, "but I'm afraid she is failing fast."

"We love the Spences very much. Their father, Dr. Will Spence, brought my mother, my brother, and myself into the world."

"What a fine tribute she paid you, Miss Clarabelle! The old people of this town must love you."

She thought fiercely to herself, Yes, yes, but I am young and I want to be loved by young people. By you!

"What a good clean sky," he said, "like your good clean eyes."

Can it be coming? she cried to herself.

They stopped at her door.

"I hope I will see you at prayer meeting tomorrow night."

"Won't you come in to supper with us?" she found herself saying.

"Say now, that *is* a thought. You're sure it will be all right?"

"More than all right."

"My mother is having dinner with friends in St. Louis to-night. I don't need to call for her until about ten. May I use your telephone to tell the girl I won't be home at the parsonage for dinner?"

Good clean eyes. He liked them good and clean, and all this time she had been wishing them blue, like Blossom

Eberhardt's. Yet here he was, liking her brown ones, because they were good and clean . . .

As deftly as she had whisked off her apron at sight of her unexpected guest, Clara mixed dumplings to add to the chicken, added fresh peas that were already hulled for the following night to her menu, and dispatched Anchutz to Daly's Food Market for ice cream and frozen raspberries, to be served along with her freshly baked cocoanut layer cake.

Throughout the meal spots of tension-red burned on Clara's cheeks. What a fortunate stroke that Clarabelle happened to have been wearing that pretty blouse when she encountered the Reverend at Miss Ollie's! What a fortunate stroke that Clarabelle had thought of taking broth over to Miss Ollie's! What a further stroke of fortune that not only had she been wearing that sheer pretty blouse, but in it had encountered the Reverend at Miss Ollie's! Might it be fate paving the way for two young people?

Ed and Anchutz accepted the visit as pleasant enough, but without implications. To such a degree, in fact, that after dinner it took some skill on Clara's part to maneuver them out of the living room, where they had adjourned for coffee in the seldom used demitasses.

"You get the darnedest notions, Clara," growled Ed, mounting the stairs after her. "What's the idea, chasing us out?"

"Wimmin will be wimmin," commented Anchutz, whistling as he descended to his basement workshop.

In the new silence the Reverend and Clarabelle regarded one another in some embarrassment.

Mama didn't need to be so obvious, thought Clarabelle.

Nevertheless, it was wonderful to be sitting beside him on the couch, in the midst of a silence that contained him.

He broke it softly. "You are a nice family, Miss Clarabelle. One of the nicest. One can feel you like as well as love one another."

She turned shining eyes. "That's a wonderful way to put it—'like as well as love one another.' I guess we've always been that way. Togetherness."

She spoke the bland word, popularized by a magazine, without awareness that she had been reached by an advertising campaign.

"In my work I see so much family antagonism, rudeness among members of the family, lack of respect, no room for God."

"Our parents brought us up close to God," she said without piousness, and the thought moved through him: This is truly a good girl. She will do well as a pastor's wife. She is a serene girl who will pray deeply and carry to the sick. This is a pure girl, and there lies her beauty.

He regarded her wistfully. When Clarabelle prayed— he had watched her many times and heard her voice sing out reverently in ensemble—some of God was in her face. A good girl, he kept repeating, as if reassuringly. As she sat there beside him so quietly, her hands interlocked, he kept brushing out of his eyes an image, thin as cobweb, of a face with very, very sky-blue eyes. . . .

They talked of church matters, the Christmas bazaar, how to enlarge Sunday-school attendance, and Clarabelle came up with what the pastor considered a splendid idea for a grandmothers' fashion show and cake-baking contest.

"I wish we had more like you in the congregation, Miss

Clarabelle. I intend to build it up, but we need workers, especially where the children and old folks are concerned. It is plain to see you have a love for both."

I have, I have. And I would work for you with all I have, said her eyes. And so would Blossom, she did not add aloud.

Why not this girl! Above everything, a man of the cloth needed a dedicated wife, a woman to understand the deep spiritual fervors within him, a woman who would bear him children. A family to rear! He found himself wanting that. Why not? His mother would depart for her home happy in this decision and this choice.

"What do you want most out of life, Clarabelle?"

She regarded him almost pointedly. "To love and be loved. To share. To be close to God."

Bless this girl. The time had come to act, to stop procrastinating, to cease letting his eyes commit the sin of wandering to the brightness of the flesh. Now.

"Clarabelle, I—I—too want to love and be loved. Let us——"

The moment between them beat like a living heart.

Into it, breathless because she had rushed five blocks to borrow them from a friend who stored Winter Beauty apples in her cellar, burst Clara, bearing a bowl of the fancy red fruit.

"I thought you two might enjoy a spot of fresh fruit. These are called Winter Beauties——" began Clara, still short of breath, and then realized that something had shattered as she entered. A moment and a mood had indeed fallen apart, as if something porcelain had crashed.

The Reverend sprang guiltily to his feet. "Thank you, no, Mrs. Sprague. I didn't realize it was so late. It's almost ten.

147

I must call for my mother. Thank you for a pleasant evening."

He was gone and, with all her control gone with him, Clarabelle sank to the couch, beating her hands into its upholstery, her stricken face twisted in dry agony.

"You ruined it! Why did you have to do it? You ruined everything. He was going to say it, I know he was—you ruined my life, that's what you've done—this is the bitter end . . ."

"Clarabelle, Clarabelle, what did Mother do?"

"Another minute—and now that minute is gone. Forever! I know it in my bones. He isn't sure enough of himself, but in that minute that you ruined he was getting sure. Oh, Mama, Mama, how could you . . ."

"My child——"

"Don't touch me!"

But Clara would not be rebuffed. On her knees beside the couch, she tried to clasp Clarabelle into her arms. There had never been a moment such as this between them, of terrible spill of emotions, of anguish unleashed.

"Clarabelle, Clarabelle, tell me what to do! I'll go to him; I'll bring him back."

"No, no, no. If you do, I'll kill myself. Spilled milk won't go back. Don't—don't—just let me be, Mama . . ."

"I wanted to make it nice for him. I thought of the apples. I know he likes apples. I rushed to Marie Busch's for them. He likes to pare them all in one piece. I remembered . . . Oh, Clarabelle, what have I done——"

"Go away, Mama. Only go away!" And the beating of Clarabelle's fists into the couch began all over again.

"He will come back, Clarabelle."

"He isn't sure enough of himself . . . and I love him . . ."

"A man doesn't fall away that easily. He will come . . ."

"He won't. I feel it in my bones! And when I feel in my bones—I know! It was the moment. Then or never. I had it almost in my hand, and I missed it. You missed it for me. Oh, Mama, how could you?"

Clara sat back on her heels and began to sob in rising rasps. God forgive me, if my child won't! Help me! Help her! Help him back! And then Clara's sobs turned into hysteria and she crammed her handkerchief into her mouth to drown the sounds that neither Ed nor Anchutz must hear.

They were terrible, and Clarabelle lifted her face to gaze down upon her mother crouched with her face dug down into the carpet.

"Mama, don't!" she cried, slipping down beside her and lifting her. "Mama, don't. I'm a beast! Beat me, Mama, hate me, slap me."

"I've ruined——"

"You're so good, and I'm no good. You did it for me. You did it for me, and I'm a beast. If he's gone, it was not to be anyway. God forgive me, Mama, I love you, Mama, I love you . . ."

They embraced in an emotional swoon that transcended all their experience.

In the basement Anchutz whistled softly as he sawed away at a plywood partition he was making for the pigeon house on Fred's roof. Upstairs, on the edge of his bathtub, Ed was paring his toenails.

Chapter 25

GOD AND HIS PRETTY ONE

ALTHOUGH SHE HAD ATTENDED WASHINGTON UNIVERSITY
in St. Louis for a year, Blossom Eberhardt taught in Miss
Tanner's Kindergarten and Nursery School.

Pretty enough in a fragile way, she had worn a succession
of fraternity pins of Washington University men, who usually eschewed coeds. Not obviously flirtatious, her popularity
excited speculation. Why Blossom, when she was not to be
mentioned, either in scholarship or beauty, with two or three
members of her class who wore no such scalps?

The eldest of four daughters of the vice-president of the
Eberhardt Construction Company, Contracting, Alterations, Modernization, she drove her own Chevrolet, shared
a separate telephone with two of her younger sisters, and
spent her slender earnings on luxury items.

The Eberhardt residence, white-pillared in the early-
American tradition, shadowed by a pair of oak trees of older
growth, stood pleasantly in the center of a wide, well-kept

lawn. Three generations of Eberhardts had lived in it, enlarged and modernized it, without designating it by name.

But within recent months one of Blossom's luxury expenditures had been for pale blue stationery, engraved "Twin Oaks."

Mrs. Eberhardt had regarded the sheet of notepaper with cocked head and an expression of pleased indulgence. Twin Oaks! What a good idea! Strange no one had thought of it before. "I'll borrow the die, Blossom, and have some notepaper of my own made up. Look, Kurt, Twin Oaks!"

But her husband had tossed it aside with a shrug. "Twin Oaks. Twin nonsense. An English lord doesn't live here."

"But Kurt, the vice-president of Eberhardt Construction Company, does."

That company in some ways resembled Twin Oaks. Old, finished with growth, its best years behind it, the president, Kurt's crotchety brother, older by eleven years, hostile to bigness and the march of time.

The design of the Kurt Eberhardt family was four girls ranging from five to twenty, the mother even smaller and daintier than her eldest, Blossom. Her large, vital husband, who over the years still retained some of his passion for her, nevertheless rushed off on every possible occasion from the monotony of her, to card playing at his club or any business pretext that would take him from home.

A brace of circumstances, including the physical satisfactions he still derived from his pretty wife, held him rigidly to the straight path of conformity, however the eyes and mind might stray. So did his church, business, and civic status and the fact that his last child, Amarylla, was a cerebral-palsy case.

The lovely-featured Amarylla, her face as bland as a saucer of milk, held this household together like an iron rivet.

Three girls deferred to her, revolved around her wheel chair, protected her from isolation. When Mrs. Eberhardt left the house for canasta, or she and her husband attended a church or social function, they kept in telephone communication with the room on the flower-garden side of the house which contained Amarylla. No one ever demurred, including the young lady of the house, Blossom, at remaining home with her on a maid's day out.

Kurt, whose pain over this child, as well as sense of guilt, lived with him, had donated in her name a larger sum of money than he could afford to a cerebral-palsy research project, his older brother, who could afford it, matching the sum.

The summer of Blossom's twentieth birthday, when the entire family had spent the month of June at Lake Louise, Canada, Amarylla in her wheel chair had traveled along, a constant, if pitiful, participant.

Bright objects or sounds from a toy horn or a spoon against a plate could capture Amarylla's attention, but seldom, if ever, the spoken word. On her birthday and at Christmas she was wheeled into the dining room, to be surrounded by her gifts and fed by spoon, the dribble ignored.

The afflicted child seemed to have it in her power to irradiate a family otherwise remarkably unremarkable. A husband and wife extended themselves far beyond themselves. Blossom, whose face, like all the Eberhardt children's, was as undisturbed as a doll's, belied her apparent passivity.

In full command of the artillery of her sex, Blossom may have graduated from high school by the skin of her teeth, but they were provocatively small, white, and pretty teeth, and when she lifted her lips to smile, they were part of the answer to what men saw in her.

Now she was caring more than she had ever cared before, in the procession of infatuations and admirers, what, if anything, Reverend Phillip Polkinhorne might be seeing in her.

The new regularity of Blossom's church attendance was a matter of amused and approving comment between Kurt Eberhardt and his wife. Hitherto, although her father's position as vice-president of the congregation made attendance more or less mandatory, her irregularity had been a matter of frequent rebuke.

At a Wednesday-evening prayer meeting Blossom picked up the fact that the Reverend had a habit of dropping in at the Spence sisters' for a spot of five-o'clock tea.

One late afternoon, shortly after the Reverend's precipitous departure from the Ed Sprague residence, Blossom, responding to a recurring impulse, bound her flowing hair with a bright ribbon and set out for the Spences' tearoom.

There she not only met Reverend Polkinhorne, but their encounter took place on the sidewalk, so that they entered together.

"Who would dream of meeting busy you here, Reverend Polkinhorne!"

"I look forward to this hour of the day for Miss Janet's tea to do a pick-me-up job on me, which it certainly does. Are you alone?"

"I certainly am."

"Suppose, then, we be alone together, and share a table?"

"I like that!"

A group of passing motorists were the sole other occupants.

Miss Janet, so eager, fluttered before the Reverend like a grounded pigeon, leading the way to a window table which overlooked a side-yard oleander tree, its heavy buds seeming to quiver in anticipation of month-off spring.

Over tea and hot jelly doughnuts an hour flew by, Reverend Polkinhorne in the grip of the pleasant excitements this pretty thing set going in him.

His thin, boyish face, slow to beard, felt flushed, although actually his habitual pallor did not budge. But behind his horn-rimmed glasses his eyes could not seem to leave her face. As Blossom moved, they moved.

"I think I know why you really come here, Reverend. For the wonderful reason you do everything. To do good. I'm sure you must be one of Miss Ollie's regular visitors upstairs."

"That is true, but my motives are also selfish. I usually plan a sermon over this cup of tea."

"Oh dear, then I am intruding!"

He leaned toward her. "The happiest intrusion I could have, Miss Blossom."

"Oh, Reverend, are you sure!"

"So sure."

"I'm a flibberty-jibberty, and you need quiet."

"I also need pleasant company."

"I don't want to sound like a schoolgirl, but you just don't know what it means to have you in the church after all these years of—of—old Reverend Beatty. Not that he wasn't just wonderful too—I mean, in a church way—but the congregation just loves you."

"I am happy here, Miss Blossom. My two previous pulpits were everything I could desire from a temporary standpoint. But from the way I feel here, I find myself hoping, God and you good people willing, I can stay and build a permanent life right here in West Grove."

"Oh, I hope so. I know so. My father is a pillar, and he keeps saying he hopes you are as happy with us as we are with you." She finished with her lips parted in a breathless gasp.

He thought her gesture of hand to throat and the thirsty little-bird manner in which her mouth opened a lovely young mannerism, and his own youth responded, a little guiltily.

Awareness of her flesh tingled through him. What he had been holding off from entering his thinking broke through. So did consciousness of the danger he had been in, only a week before, in attempting to force himself into accepting what was not the real thing.

Blossom was beautiful. She was bright as honey. He wanted her to bear his children, God forgive him for the urgencies of the flesh. Unconsciously his hand felt for the small Bible he carried in his coat pocket, closed tightly around it. God forgive him . . .

They chatted inconsequentially through another serving of jelly doughnuts. She licked a spot of jam off her finger, as a child would, and yet she had maturity, a certain something which he could not define, a look of knowing a great many things.

How often he had talked to his mother about the need of a young pastor for just this kind of wife, who could walk beside him with sympathy and understanding! This pretty creature had both, in addition to that strange kind of maturity he could not quite capture.

It was dawning on him that she was not all child. If only

he had realized it before the conclusion of his mother's visit just two days ago!

She had never voiced opposition to Blossom. But her inclination had always seemed to lean in the direction of Clarabelle. To think he had been so perilously close to doing that nice girl the monstrous injustice of interpreting his liking for her as something more!

It had taken this lovely creature across the table from him, within reach of him, to make him realize what Mrs. Sprague's providential interruption had averted for both himself and her fine daughter, Clarabelle. Or had God's finger been pointing the way?

Yet even now caution stood at his elbow, and a great haste suddenly possessed him and he looked at his watch and told Blossom it had been a pleasant hour.

They walked together beneath trees that appeared still broody with winter, but within them the sap of spring was already due to rise. Within sight of her home, it came as he suspected it might.

"It is proper, isn't it," she asked, "to invite the pastor in to dinner?"

"And it is proper," he replied, against his caution, "for the pastor to mingle with his flock, when and wherever possible."

"Then won't you come to our house?" she said with a curtsy and the tip of her forefinger charmingly to her chin.

No question about it, "pretty thing" was the phrase for her, he said inwardly.

Mrs. Eberhardt had not yet returned from a canasta afternoon nor her husband from his office.

The younger girls, in red jackets and red woolly caps,

played about the lawn with neighborhood children and ran to greet their older sister with kisses and curtsies for the Reverend.

Indoors, the living room, refurnished upon Blossom's graduation, might have been designed to harmonize with her blondness. As a matter of fact, it had been. Copied verbatim from the illustrated pages of *Modern Interior Magazine*, footsteps sank silently into the deep nap of cream-colored wall-to-wall carpet. Pale mahogany chairs and outsize sofas, upholstered in faint gold, stood at studied equidistance, a brilliant but meaningless abstract painting above a stylized fireplace lending planned contrast to the honey-colored scheme. Beyond this room the house relaxed into the pleasantly shabby décor of no period in particular and of several periods in general.

Reverend Polkinhorne had previously been a dinner guest here with his mother, but he had never beheld it irradiated by a sunset visible from the picture window. Like the majority of the dwelling places of his parishioners, this house was typical of the warmth of the family life of the community to which he had so fortuitously fallen heir.

Blossom left him for a brief dash into the kitchen to appraise the colored cook of the important acquisition of the Reverend for dinner.

When she returned he was standing beside the piano, regarding a framed photograph of the four Eberhardt girls.

"What a beautiful group!"

"Oh, that. It's terrible of me."

"It is beautiful of you, Blossom," he said softly, lingering along the name as if it were a sweet. "But I don't believe I ever saw this little blond doll looking over your shoulder. She must have been in bed when I was around. Except for the difference in age, you might be twins."

"That is my baby sister, Amarylla. She's our darling little invalid. Come and meet her; she's even prettier than her picture."

In an adjoining sunroom, bright toys around her, Amarylla, propped up in her chair, was being fed her supper by a young Negro maid who tilted the spoon between her lips.

"Tammie, may we interrupt? I want the Reverend to see Amarylla."

"She's been waiting for you, Miss Blossom."

The child in the chair turned her heart-shaped face, her lips parted for a succession of little bleats, and Blossom's identical smile shone through.

"That means Amarylla is happy to see us, Reverend Polkinhorne," said Blossom without further explanation. "Amarylla understands a great deal, doesn't she, Tammie?"

"That child knows more than anybody thinks, Pastor."

"May I shake hands with her?"

"Indeed you may," interposed Blossom, hastily lifting the dimpled hand and placing it in the Reverend's. "She is happy to meet you, aren't you, darling? See how she smiles?"

The Reverend looked into the blazingly blue motionless eyes, empty of expression.

"Indeed I do," he replied, holding the child's still hand.

"I declare, Miss Blossom, this child knows when you are on your way home ten minutes before you get there."

"She knows I never forget her, don't you, darling? See what Sister has brought you today."

She opened her handbag and produced a round pink mint. "Candy from the Spences' tearoom for you. . . . She likes pink, Reverend. I gave her a pair of little pink slippers for her birthday and she smiled, didn't she, Tammie?"

"Yes, ma'am. Amarylla smiles more for you than anybody."

"I love her so, Reverend," said Blossom, regarding him with moist eyes. "I just love her so."

He was moved. This was beautiful! The compassion in the eyes of this wonderful girl for a child God had not quite finished. How had he ever hesitated or debated! This girl could walk beside him among his people. This wonderful, wonderful girl. Would she give him yes?

Back once more in the living room, he took her without preamble into his arms. Their lips met, merged. If only his mother had not departed for Davenport. . . .

The weight of her relaxed body swayed against him.

How could he ever be sufficiently thankful for this girl? That look on her face as she had regarded Amarylla. If only his mother could have seen it!

He had never been so close to possessing a woman before. Intimations of his unrealized self crowded into the moment. Simultaneously he felt the need to prolong his ecstasy and the need to pray, to expiate for what was not sin and yet— somehow—a sense of guilt intruded.

"My pretty one," he whispered against her hair, "I must ask your parents for you tonight. We will telephone to my mother in Davenport. We must be married soon, soon."

"Soon, Phillip?"

"Oh, my dear, say the name again."

Phillip.

Again and again.

Phillip, Phillip, my love.

Reverend Polkinhorne prayed through most of that night, his thoughts deeply with his God and his pretty one.

Chapter 26

SHE WAS MISTRESS HERE

VIRGIE'S ORIENTATION TO HER NEW WORLD WAS NOT WITH-out its rough spots. But outweighing the difficulties were some of the sharpest pleasures she had ever experienced.

Morning after morning she would awaken, lie for a moment until the reality of her new life took slow shape, then stretch out her hand for the further reality of Charley lying beside her.

Once she shook him gently awake. "Charley, wake up. I'm so happy, I want you to know it."

"Go back to sleep, baby," he said without opening his eyes and flinging an arm across her body as he slid back into it himself.

It was wonderful to watch him asleep, to behold their handsome bedroom slowly emerge out of dawn's early light. Her clothes folded over the back of the pale brocade chair beside her bed. Their bed. This was their room, their home. She was mistress here.

161

Mistress. The word smote her. They were married before God! They had spoken their oaths before Him. Dear, dear Charley.

She regarded him as he lay, his curved back toward her, before she too slipped back to sleep.

The days raced! In no time Virgie had taken over, rousing the house from its deep lethargy of the long-time womanless regime, filling it with the momentum of the lady of the house in action. Rugs to the renovators, to come back bright with colors that had long been sunk deeply into the nap. New hangings. The sparkle restored to crystal chandeliers and mahogany surfaces. This table over there. Out with that chair. Down with those hangings. Out with that fusty lampshade. More bowls for flowers. Who wanted cracked-looking smoky mirrors, just because they were antique? New shiny ones!

On hands and knees Virgie waxed linoleum; hung gingham curtains; arranged potted geraniums on the kitchen window sills. Bed- and bathrooms were rejuvenated, including Brock's long-unused suite in which he was now installed.

Charley's released spirits roared through the house.

By golly, the woman has all but scoured the ceilings! What's this in my bathroom? A scale, so I can watch my belly. He whacked her through her thin negligee so that the flesh rang. "Don't you go losing yours! I like my girl with meat on her."

You could be coarse with this woman in the natural way. Bring home stories from the bars and smoking room and encounter not squeamishness but camaraderie and good humor as noisy as his own.

But only when they were alone. In the presence of Brock,

the aged cook, or the part-time housemaid, Virgie coated herself over with lady-of-the-house.

Uppermost in her mind there persisted the certainty that Charley, sparring for time, must face the inevitability of inviting his brothers and their families to meet her.

"Honey, please don't let me interfere with your family relations. I'll understand if they don't take to me."

"They're rarin' to come."

"Why not ask them, Charley?"

"Waiting to get the house all fixed up."

She sat on his lap and locked hands around his neck. "Charley, don't be ashamed to be ashamed of me."

He dumped her unceremoniously. "Crazy in the head! Ashamed! If truth be known, I'm ashamed of them. Whether they like you or not, so what! Just you go up to Brock's rooms and ask him whether he likes you or not. Lucky for me he didn't meet you first."

"But Brock is different, honey. Brock needs somebody like me—around——"

"So do I, and how! I told Claudia last week we were going to invite the family in."

"Then let's get it over with, honey. I don't want to be the one to keep a family apart."

"All right. Say when."

"Week from Saturday?"

"Week from Saturday."

Chapter 27

A WEEK FROM SATURDAY

GOOD HUMOR AND PLEASANTRIES PREVAILED. FOUR COUSINS, Brock and Claudia, Anchutz and Clarabelle, scarcely more than strangers, showed amiability. Even Ed displayed little of his separateness. Myra performed a brace of Chopin études, and Virgie accomplished an evening memorable in the annals of a not too cohesive family.

The excellent home dinner was largely prepared by Virgie.

"Just like that," explained Charley with a snap of his fingers. "Wouldn't know she was doing it, except when the smell of onions French-frying and cakes baking began to smell up the place like delicious heaven."

"I was raised next to work," smiled Virgie, her bosom, rounded as a pouter pigeon's, rising and falling rapidly.

"The woman all but washes and irons my folding money."

"I like to iron. It smooths out my temper."

"She's got none to smooth," expanded Charley, glancing pridefully from one to the other.

164

At this point Virgie could have let go a rip-roaring anecdote if she and Charley had been alone. She would save it for the privacy of their bedroom.

What Charley could not get over, as he later confided to Virgie, was the thawing process of Ed and his wife. They defrosted. Even daughter Clarabelle, whose face, on those rare occasions when the families met, always appeared stiff as china. Cousins acted like cousins. "And, Virgie, that was a swell thing you did about the magnum of champagne."

What Virgie did was to substitute quarts for the extra-sized bottles which Charley had set cooling in the ice buckets.

"What's the idea, honey?" Charley had roared at the table. "Where's the magnums? Quarts won't wet up this celebration."

In the silence, freighted with the awareness of things being the way they were, Brock, tall, pale, and unembarrassed, rose from his chair and in more of the unprecedented spirit of the occasion walked down the lavish length of the table and kissed Virgie on her high bosom where it bulged above the décolleté line.

As if this were not sufficient for an evening that rose upon itself like a pyramid, Brock moved over to the silver buckets on their stands beside his father, opened two bottles with a minimum of fizz, and passed around the table, pouring. At his own place he picked up his goblet, held it aloft, empty, and crashed it to pieces with the handle of his knife.

To his own and to general amazement, Ed found himself on his feet, lifting his glass. Everyone followed suit.

To the bride and groom!

Virgie, with her throat tight, looked about the table and down its length.

These were her brothers-in-law and sisters-in-law, her nieces and nephews. She was one of them. The Spragues of St. Louis and West Grove.

All these were Charley's people, and therefore her people. She was one of them. Inside a family circle. The Sprague circle.

Chapter 28

NO SUMMER

BLOSSOM MARIE EBERHARDT AND PHILLIP STONE POLKIN-horne were about to be married on the lawn of Rock Church. A classmate of Reverend Polkinhorne's had come from his pastorate in Biloxi, Mississippi, to perform the ceremony.

It was one of those perfect June days when nature herself behaves like a bride, decking herself in the accouterments of first flowerings.

Almost an entire congregation, including the three Sprague families, were likewise decking themselves for the high-noon function.

Myra, limbering up her fingers by running them in arpeggios up and down the surface of her dressing table, was ready and waiting for John Henry to finish dressing.

Years of West Grove brides and grooms had gone to their marriage altars to the strains of her rendition of the "Wedding March." Presently, as she struck forth Mendelssohn from the small organ that would be rolled to the church porch, Blossom and Phillip would proceed across the green turf.

Only the week previous, Myra had played this wedding march in an East St. Louis synagogue, for the daughter of her old friends Mr. and Mrs. Hyman Shalom. She had worn the same expensive, well-made brown taffeta, the matching spot of an expensive, not too becoming, brown hat. No summer in either. For that matter, one could have wondered, had there ever been summer in Myra?

Through the open door of John Henry's room across the hall she could hear him fuming over a certain collar button essential to the shirt he wore with his usher's striped pants and cutaway. It had slipped through his fingers and, swearing none too softly, he was crawling on all fours, peering beneath furniture and behind drapes. An inclination both to laugh and cry stirred within carefully contained Myra. Need life be so tasteless or—ridiculous? Would it be different if she were married to a man with whom she had sufficient in common to keep alive the private and splendid excitements? Or must marriage mean diminishing exhilarations and communication, unfulfillment, compromise?

Take her new sister-in-law. Myra would have wagered that the sweet, hussy-looking creature with the knocked-about look to her took life as it came. Why couldn't she? Myra may have had her own judgments concerning Virgie, but you had to admire what appeared to be Virgie's philosophy: You've made your bed. Lie on it. Well, at least Virgie must do that to the satisfaction of Charley, who could not keep his hands off her.

But she was certainly one sweet person. Common, perhaps. No man would dare whack a woman, even his wife, on the backside on every possible occasion unless she were a certain kind of woman. John Henry must have sensed it too, because he had once bored his forefinger into Virgie's cheek and said, "Dimple-dimple," in baby talk, mind you!

No, the Sprague brothers were not exactly irresistibles, mused Myra as she contemplated her husband crawling about the floor.

She never quite dared ask herself whether she had married John Henry for his money. There were so many escape reasons involved. Certainly his financial status had not been a liability. But strangely, the pick of the three brothers, when it came to a certain something not easily definable, was Ed, who stood off on his own through the years, never for an instant toadying to Charley, the way John Henry had. And now Myra had somehow let the toadying happen to her. They both catered to the side their bread was buttered and jellied on.

She continued to watch John Henry crawling about the floor.

Chapter 29

GOD HAD BEEN
JUST AS CLOSE
ON PINE STREET

THE EBERHARDT-POLKINHORNE WEDDING WAS THE SEC-
ond for Virgie during her residence in West Grove, where
her social integration had been slow.

Virgie's own wedding to Scogan, so remote, had taken
place in a town hall which consisted of two rooms over a
feed store in an adjoining town called Fancy Prairie, where
they had gone to be married by a sheriff who doubled as
justice of the peace.

The first marriage she had attended in West Grove had
taken place in January, and Virgie could cry at the mere recol-
lection. Organ music had rolled over the well-dressed guests.
A row of Spragues had sat well up front, in the family pew
with the family name engraved on a metal plate across the
back.

The bride and groom had been strangers to her, but her
tears had been copious. These lovely wedding trappings had
been missing for her and Charley, but God had been just

as close as they had spoken their vows before the window in that little room on Pine Street. She wept as a woman weeps, for joy and for sorrow. Her tears as she gazed upon the West Grove wedding scene had been for the swift passing of the youth of these strangers, for the brief moment of sanctity in the church, for the realities awaiting them beyond its portals, and the invading thought that one day, again to flowers and roll of organ, these two, the splendor of youth turned into grays, would be horizontal before an altar in the rigidity of death. But once again in the presence of God . . .

Now, dressing herself for the Eberhardt-Polkinhorne wedding, Virgie zippered herself into a pink print dress and adjusted a somewhat too droopy leghorn hat with two large pink roses wreathing it.

Under no conditions would she weep at this wedding and splotch up her face.

Chapter 30

WHAT DO I CARE?

EVERY BEDROOM IN ED SPRAGUE'S HOUSE WAS AGOG AND IN motion. Clara had wanted Anchutz to have a white jacket for this June wedding on the lawn, and had offered to pay half herself, but Anchutz had been adamant.

"Cripes, isn't it enough I have to show up at all? The last thing I want is to give up a Saturday afternoon to a wedding, of all things."

"You should want to go if for no other reason than your father's status in the church, to say nothing of the fact that it happens to be the wedding of your pastor."

"Aren't three members of the family enough? The Sprague tribe is sure to attend, and that means Mr. and Mrs. Oil meet Mr. and Mrs. Water."

"Now, Anchutz, your Uncle Charley's new wife has changed all that quite a bit; you've admitted as much yourself."

"She's a good egg, but one good egg doesn't make a basket of them."

"Don't forget to take off those tan shoes, son—your black ones are next to your bed—and have the car out of the garage, so your father doesn't have to do it, and see to it that the back seat isn't cluttered with your fishing paraphernalia. Your sister and I are wearing new clothes."

"You look immense, Mom."

"Wait until you see your sister!"

"What'll you bet she doesn't want this shindig any more than I do, and what'll you bet Pop don't," quipped Anchutz, kissing his mother and bounding around to the garage.

Like a hole in the head, Anchutz told himself, that's how much I want to go. Not a comfortable moment while his Uncle Charley was around. Always made a fellow feel a failure. Not by what he said or did, but somehow he made you think of money, his money. It stuck out of his ears. Give him his Uncle John Henry every time—that is, without Aunt Myra, who looked as ill at ease with life as he was sure to feel at Polkinhorne's wedding.

"If only Anchutz would take more interest in these affairs," Clara reiterated to her husband. "But such matters roll off that boy like water off a duck's back. He's never even been in calf love."

Backing the car out of the garage, Anchutz was wondering if, following the wedding, his father would be disposed to spend the remainder of the afternoon finishing that kitchen cabinet they were making for Mom.

Glancing out of her window, Clarabelle could see her brother backing out of the garage. It must be time! The clock on her table showed half past eleven. Fifteen minutes left to herself before starting for the high-noon ceremony.

She stood dressed before her mirror. In certain ways her glasses did enhancing things to her eyes, magnifying them slightly. Clarabelle did little for her clothes, wearing them with no distinction, and they in turn did little for her.

But her blue organza frock was becoming, its sash emphasizing her slim waist. Her mother had made the blue hat with cornflowers peeping through tulle. It could have been lovely. It was not bad on Clarabelle.

Ten minutes more!

Under the stress she spoke aloud to herself.

What am I afraid of? What do I care? A man who can see anything in her certainly isn't the man for me to see anything in. I should be glad. I am, and I'm glad I'm me, home here with Mama and Papa and my own little room with my own little job. She's no more fit to be a minister's wife than our canary. Imagine her at the Ladies Auxiliary or organizing a Christmas bazaar. I'm well out of it, except that—fool that I am. Thank God nobody knows except Mama and me. Not even Anchutz has the slightest idea what it is all about.

No minutes more!

Her mother's voice came up the stairs as it had been winding up to her through her lifetime.

"Clarabelle," she cried too gaily, "time to start, dear!"

"Coming, Mom!" called back Clarabelle too gaily, taking up her new white gloves and handbag with a little cluster of cornflowers embroidered on it.

Down in the living room her father was struggling into his coat.

"Oh, Ed, doesn't Clarabelle look sweet!"

She stood on the stairs, inviting inspection.

"She sure does. Clarabelle, you look as pretty as a picture."

"That, coming from your father, means something."

"It certainly does, Papa."

"Now don't go flirting with the boys today. I want you for my girl."

"You hear," cried Clara, her high-voiced gaiety accelerating, "your father wants you for his girl, and I don't blame him, the way you look in that blue outfit!"

The darlings, she cried inwardly, the darlings, trying to make it easy for me. Oh, Mama, Papa, I love you so, but let me alone . . .

"Clarabelle, don't change your clothes after the wedding. We're going for a drive out to Ciccardi's for supper, just the four of us."

"That's a fine idea!" exclaimed Ed, who notoriously disliked restaurants.

Suddenly Clarabelle in all her finery turned her face against the wall and laid her head in the curve of her arm.

"Don't feel sorry for me. Stop it. I can't bear it. Go away, please go away, please. Just leave me be . . ."

The hat with the cornflowers fell backward on her head and she snuggled deeper and deeper into the crook of her arm. "Go, go, only don't feel sorry for me . . ."

In their bewilderment and alarm, Clara and Ed stood exchanging transfixed stares. When Clara started toward the figure against the wall, Ed stopped her with a forefinger across his lips, and so they continued to stand watching the anguish of their daughter and waiting for the storm to pass.

After a while it was Ed who went over and laid a hand on Clarabelle's shoulder.

"Come, daughter," he said softly, "you're going to feel better now. Let your mother fix your hat and dry off your face a bit. One more tear out of you two and I'll whack you both."

Compliantly mustering a smile, Clarabelle swung around, holding her lips as firm as she could manage while her mother kept saying, "That's fine," and helped adjust the hat and found her powder compact and touched up the blotches. "That's fine. That's just fine."

"For cripes' sake, what's the hitch in there?" shouted Anchutz from the driveway. "Get a move on or they will be an old married couple by the time we get there."

"Hold your horses," cried Clarabelle, "here we come!"

Chapter 31

COME UP TO BED, BABY

CHARLEY AND VIRGIE HAD FALLEN INTO THE AFTER-DIN-
ner habit of tucking themselves into a small room that ad-
joined the kitchen. It had served first as maid's room, then
as children's dining room for Claudia and Brock, and in the
latter years as a repository for unused luggage and miscella-
neous overflow.

A small fireplace, which had probably never been used,
was what caught Virgie's eye. On the strength of it she had
refurbished the room out of oddments of chairs and tables,
papered, painted, and curtained it, until it emerged a little
pocket of warm privacy into which they both liked to retreat,
attired for bed, especially as the evenings lengthened and
the going fireplace made sparking sounds.

The matter of conformity in clothes was not easy for
Virgie. Women in her new world did not wear negligees beyond the bedroom—and certainly not at dinner—or change
from street clothes into them the moment they arrived in-

doors. Virgie did. She had lived that way too long, inside the cocoon of her flat in Pine Street, the latchstring out, herself always in.

As a matter of fact, Charley preferred her way. His sister-in-law's hint to him that he might mention to Virgie that it was wiser to slip into a dress for dinner even when they were alone went unheeded.

Virgie in dishabille was the Virgie he had known from the beginning. It gave him a deep sense of her being at home, particularly at twilight and evening.

After all, they were enjoying twilight years together, even though her twilight was years behind his.

He liked her precisely the way she was. And the way she was included her good nature, sunniness, easy surrender in bed, her relish of the kind of joke a man could not bring home to every woman. Imagine Myra or Clara!

Often they sat in contented silence, listened to radio, or played stud poker for stakes that were never paid.

If Brock were home to dinner, as he was with growing frequency, he joined them afterward, but seldom to remain longer than the length of a cigarette—and then out to the garage for his car, or back to his rooms.

Charley was relieved at these departures and said so. "Brock is nobody's fool. He knows I have been without you all my life and that every minute alone with you is coming to me. We're still bride and groom. We'll always be. . . ."

She kissed him with even more fervency than usual, and he sensed why. A man and his wife!

But she rebuked him gently. "Charley, that boy of yours is fighting a battle. I've had enough experiences with men and women fighting it. He needs this home; he needs you."

"You mean he needs you," growled Charley and pinched her. "He can have anything I've got except my privacy with my girl."

"He doesn't want that, Charley. All he wants is help."

"I don't want to bother your head about it, but I break my own trying to figure him out."

"When he comes out of those spells of locking himself up in his room, Charley, I have yet to smell alcohol on him. Those bottles in his room stay full-up instead of drunk-down."

"Not a drinking man in my family or—Polly's—and yet—it's the way with solitary drinkers. I don't intend to stand by much longer and guess. It's time to barge in."

She laid a quick hand on his arm. "Wait just a while longer, Charley. That boy may be in the middle of being hard hit by something no one knows about. A love affair——"

"Don't worry, he's off women after the lesson he had."

"Maybe off again until he's on again, perhaps for the better this time."

"No, talking of remarriage to him is like waving a red flag. I warned him against the one bad mistake he made. This time he is warning himself against another."

"The boy needs help of some kind."

"He's against psychiatrists—calls them head-shrinkers. Says they are sicker than their patients."

"What can be ailing that boy!"

"Darnedest thing. Sulks off by himself and then shows up as if nothing had happened. I tell you, no matter what you say, it looks like solitary drinking to me."

"Then we mustn't leave him solitary."

"He's got the run of the house, same as we have."

"I know it, honey. You certainly aren't being rough on him and making matters worse, like some fathers might."

"You're a godsend to him."

"I've done a lot of mothering in my time, not that my own boy gave me much chance. Family tightness is family rightness, no matter what. I never realized it until my boy dropped out of sight on me. After all, what is there in life, Charley, except ties with other human beings?"

"Thank God those ties bind you and me. Close."

"I don't mean just us, but all of you Spragues."

"Don't fool yourself, Virgie; they've no real truck with me. The Ed Spragues have stood off from me as if what I wanted to give them was a contagious disease."

"That's their nature."

"I gave Ed the same chance to get in on the ground floor of my first big deal that I gave John Henry."

"He was afraid to risk his savings, Charley."

"Savings, my hind foot! So were they John Henry's savings."

"Ed had young ones."

"Don't try to cover him. Even when I tried to make it easier for him, he wanted none of it."

"Whatever your folks may think of me, Charley, I can take. But I want them to think everything of you and you of them."

"This is the way it's been and this is the way I've got to like it," he replied, a grim look stiffening his face.

"What this family needs is plenty, only I'm not the one to do it. You are. It must come from you, Charley."

"I missed the boat with them."

"Take that little wet-looking sparrow, your brother Ed's daughter, Clarabelle. No girl needs to look like that. No shine to her except her nose."

"Ed's kids are like their Dad. Chicken-feed folks."

"Maybe so, with the boy. But that girl is starving to death as surely as if she didn't get enough to eat."

"I've seen homelier by far than Clarabelle, but the minute she's out of my sight I can't for the life of me remember what she looks like."

"You know what?" ruminated Virgie, chin in palm. "Funny how things pop into your mind—that Mrs. Schlachter next door who rents out her first floor to the Christian Science Reading Room and who has called on me twice— that's a mighty fine boy of hers——"

"Carl Schlachter," said Charley innocently. "Fine fellow and first-rate certified public accountant. I've called him in on a few matters."

"Certainly funny it hasn't occurred to me before," pursued Virgie.

"What?"

"Those two."

"What two?"

"Nothing, Charley."

"Guess what I'm thinking about?"

"What?"

"Bed. Come up to bed, baby—now!"

181

Chapter 32

COME UP TO BED, BABY

As Christmas approached, Virgie was experiencing her own little twinges. For so many years she had held her own kind of celebration down on Pine Street.

By contrast, the holiday at the Spragues was linked to no traditional observances. Aside from the grayish wreath of artificial holly which Katy stored away from year to year and hooked onto the front door each Christmas, the Sprague dwelling, in contrast to decorated lawns and façades along the street, stood unadorned. This year Virgie had hung bright new wreaths in each window and added red satin bows.

But on this Christmas Eve, Brock did not even arrive for turkey and mince-pie dinner, and afterward Virgie and Charley played canasta until a fairly early bedtime.

But beside Charley's plate were gold monogrammed cuff links in a ribbon-bound box, and a gaily wrapped package also awaited Brock.

Charley looked sheepish over his and rose from his place

to kiss her. "Your old man is a punk, baby. Just didn't think to do the same. We've never done much about Christmas, not even in Polly's or the kids' days. You mad at me, honey? I'll buy you anything you say."

He leaned over her chair and she wound her arms up backward, tilting her foreshortened face to his kisses. "There just couldn't be any better Christmas for me, Charley, than having you."

He kept stroking and kissing the top of her head. "Never mind, I've got my own kind of Christmas in store for you, Virgie. It can't be any finer or handsomer than these elegant cuff links, but it's going to mean a lot to you."

"I've already more than is coming to me, Charley. You!"

"One of these days we'll go down to the lawyer's together. I'm going to rewrite my will. Can you guess why? I want you to know just where you stand."

"Yes, Charley."

"You'll see. I'll make up for tonight, honey—big! We're going down to the lawyer's, and don't you forget it."

But before the holiday week was over, Virgie had "silvered up the season," as she put it, mounting a tree, its branches loaded with glitter, in the center of the living room and inviting the family to nine-o'clock eggnog.

The guests, as they unwrapped the gifts beneath the silvered tree, applauded Virgie's skill in hitting upon their various idiosyncrasies. A child's toolbox for Anchutz. Collection basket for John Henry. Toy piano, of course, for Myra. Papier-mâché quail for Charley. And so went the gaiety.

Alex, the hired part-time community butler, dispensed

eggnog and mixed drinks. A silvered cornucopia spilled grapes, strawberries, pomegranates, figs. The three brothers toasted three wives.

Later in the evening, following a church bazaar, Reverend Polkinhorne and his wife arrived, Blossom clutching a large white woolly bear which she had won in a raffle. Mrs. Schlachter and her son Carl, neighbors, also invited for a late snack, followed, and still later Claudia, with a Mr. J. Harrison Smith, obviously younger by years, in tow, whom she introduced as a "terrific expert on taxes and things."

Brock, pale, handsome, the only man in formal attire, and by now belligerently drunk, was in constant motion, talking incessantly, rapidly, angrily. "Watch your step, big boy! Who do you think you are? Oh, it's you, Anchutz. I could sneeze that name anywhere. Lay off me, Dad. You too, Virgie."

Myra, to divert the strain, played Christmas carols, the group gathering around to sing. Virgie dispatched Clarabelle and Carl to the kitchen for the silvered baskets of Christmas cakes.

Suddenly Brock, attempting to lean against the swinging door which led into the pantry, was banged into by the aging butler entering from the pantry side with a tray of glasses.

"Goddamn!" he screamed, going all the way wild, "who are you? Are you me? Answer or by God I'll grind your face into that broken glass."

Old Alex, bewildered, kneeled amidst the shattered mess. "Sorry, Mr. Brock, I didn't know you were there——"

"To hell with your apology. To hell with you."

"You don't owe anyone an apology, Alex," interceded Charley, pale from holding back anger. "Get out and get some air, Brock. You're stinking drunk."

"Hell, who says anybody owes me anything? Not a dime. That was me banging into me. That's me down there in broken glass. God in heaven, there's two of me in this hell room."

"Pull yourself together, Brock," whispered Virgie. "Pull hard."

"Get out!" thundered Charley. "Get out!"

Just as suddenly as he had exploded, Brock subsided to a whimper. "I'm sorry. God, I'm sorry, Alex. Dad—Virgie— everybody. Kick me for being a punk."

It was well after midnight before the last of them departed and Charley turned furiously on his son. "Damnation! You made a fine fool of yourself and of us all."

"Charley, please."

"Lay off me, Dad, I'm still ugly——"

"Why the hell couldn't you get tight like a gentleman?" blasted Charley, who was that way himself. "Christmas or no Christmas, men who get drunk like you are pigs and belong in the same pen with them."

"I'm warning you, Dad, cut it out," reiterated Brock, his eyes the red of railroad lanterns.

Virgie laid a restraining hand. "Boys, all this will keep until tomorrow. Charley, please! Let Brock get fresh air into him, and we'll turn out the lights. Go, Brock."

But it was two o'clock before they finally extinguished the last of the lights, leaving only one burning in the hall for Brock.

"The whole damn family had to be in on it."

"Please, Charley, let's not talk about it any more."

"An eyeful and an earful for the whole damn family."

"You've said that again and again, Charley. They've seen

young fellows loaded before, especially on holidays. Wait until tomorrow. Please, Charley—I can't listen to it any more——"

"You're tired, baby. You pulled a good party."

"Yes, but what will you bet we are all glad it's over!"

"I spoke at least a hundred words to Ed tonight. That's more than in the last I don't know how many years."

"Boy, wasn't that a specimen Claudia brought along! Help her get her own man back, Charley, or she's on the skids."

"Help her! You forget, I'm only her father."

"But you must admit, honey, even Claudia and Clarabelle had their heads together. Two heads that never before did more than nod to each other."

"No more post-mortems, baby, this Brock thing has washed me up—bone-tired and heartsick——"

"My poor Charley."

"Come up to bed, baby. I want to go to bed, Virgie. With you!"

186

Chapter 33

HE DID IT ON HIS OWN

Virgie, once so slim and long-stemmed, had spread through the years and the hips. The effect seemed to shorten her, although above the waistline she had kept some of the slender grace of her earlier figure.

Nowadays her dresses, purchased as always off the racks of popular-priced stores, required the letting out of seams.

It did not occur to Charley, who was not niggardly, to suggest that she improve her wardrobe. The half-revealing, half-concealing negligees, sufficient unto themselves, were exciting and desirable. It was gratifying to him that he was still capable of that kind of excitement.

Since he had not suggested that she improve both the quality and quantity of her wardrobe, Virgie, although secretly longing to emulate some of Claudia's elegance, nevertheless continued her patronage of the shops that sold off the racks.

Not that Charley would have demurred; she sensed that.

But she was diffident in the matter of money. He preferred the charge system, even to the grocer and butcher bills, and she shrank from the idea of expenditures larger than those to which she had been accustomed coming to his desk each month. She had yet to own her first fur coat. She knew that mink came high but was appalled, when she shopped, to find how far she had been from realizing how high. She compromised by purchasing, out of her own little store of savings from her income which had accumulated since her marriage, an imitation chinchilla jacket.

"Do you like it, Charley?" she asked, hoping it might stir him to realizations.

"I like you in it," he said, looking only into her eyes.

It was no use. She turned her thoughts in the direction of other devices. Claudia would have been her choice, but she faltered at the thought of her general remoteness. She resolved to try one day to feel sufficiently informal with Myra or Clarabelle, or even Clara, to ask them where they purchased their clothes and hats. Not that they could lay claim to distinction, or even approach the chic of Claudia, but even by comparison to theirs, her own materials felt and looked sleazy, the wools and silks inferior, and her clothes in general more bizarre than theirs in cut and color.

But before even approaching them she half resolved to buy in the departments of better clothes, instead of in bargain basements.

She would also have enjoyed some good jewelry. Myra wore handsome diamond clip earrings, a fairly large diamond ring inside her wedding band, and a wrist watch with tiny diamonds encircling it.

"In the near future," Charley had remarked the first

month of their "marriage," "I want to take you to the vault and give you some jewelry of Polly's. You'll have first choice, and Claudia and Clarabelle, who already have a great deal of it, can divide the rest between them."

She made no attempt to conceal her pleasure. "Do you think I'll know how to act, Charley? Me in the real thing!" There was something about genuine jewelry! Her own gold wedding ring, an old-fashioned wide band, she had always doubted, because it had left a greenish shade on her finger in the days when she had worn it.

Apparently Charley had not thought to suggest a gold band for her. The evening of the family dinner she had been tempted, but thought better of it, to resurrect her own wedding ring, which she kept locked away in a small box along with a yellowing photograph of Grant, waving a teething ring, the emerald and diamond brooch, and a few jewelry oddments mostly out of repair and of little sentimental or real value.

Carl Schlachter's mother, with whom she was now on running-in-and-out terms, once remarked, as she helped Virgie remove her brown cloth coat with the well-worn red fox collar, "What you need is a nice fur coat, either mink or seal. Who are you two going to leave all your money to? My Carl has a friend in the fur-storage business who can help you get it wholesale. Clarabelle just bought the nicest little American broadtail jacket from him. So reasonable. Have you seen it?"

"No." Virgie might have added, We haven't that kind of relationship.

A man named Edward Droon, one-time head of Droon Brothers, Furriers, St. Louis, who had drifted down into Pine

Street during a terrible period in his life and whom she had sobered up, had once promised her a mouton jacket. He had drifted away and with him the promise made in a gush of gratitude.

One day, browsing in one of the town's principal department stores, she encountered Clarabelle.

"The office where I work is just across the street. I cut through this store on my way to lunch and sometimes to do a little shopping. You at it too?"

"I'm selecting a sweater-vest for your Uncle Charley."

Clarabelle was wearing the new fur jacket. It was as unremarkable as Clarabelle herself, but fitted nicely, the navy-blue dress, the small matching hat, bespeaking the look of gentility which Virgie was beginning to covet.

"You look so nice, Clarabelle. Where do you get your dresses?"

Unaccustomed to complimentary observations, Clarabelle flushed. "Oh, thank you. I get them right here, up in the Casual Department. Miss Weiner always waits on me."

That was the word, *casual*. The women in West Grove wore casual clothes. And so, come to think about it, did most of them on the St. Louis streets. Slacks and simple dresses were worn indoors, flowing peignoirs, if at all, chiefly in the bedroom. Virgie intended to discipline herself to like it that way.

In the oversize red fox collar and cuffs and oversize trimmed hat which the winds pulled at, Virgie felt sufficient passing discomfort to override, momentarily at least, apprehensions and timidity.

"I guess they are pretty expensive here."

"We always find it pays in the long run to buy the best. But you certainly don't need to worry about cost."

"No, of course not. I guess. I don't suppose you would have time to come upstairs to the Casual Department with me and help me pick out a dress?"

Still warmed under praise, Clarabelle glanced at her wrist. "Yes, if we hurry."

Virgie tried on several dresses, finally reducing her selection to a choice between two: a navy-blue wool jersey and a sternly tailored tweed suit.

"Which do you prefer, Clarabelle?"

"I like them both. Take the two; they answer different purposes."

"How much are they?"

The saleswoman read the tags. "The dress is seventy-nine-fifty, the suit one hundred and twenty-five. You won't regret taking them both."

"I don't think I want to spend that much—for either. I'm sorry, Clarabelle." She still pronounced the name diffidently. "I guess I should have asked the price first."

"Why, Virgie, you should have them! Surely Uncle Charley would want you to."

"Oh yes, he would. But for my purpose, I just don't need——"

"Have them sent home on approval. That's what I do."

Under the pressure, Virgie assented, determining then and there that they would be returned unopened.

It was dear of Clarabelle to show interest, and Virgie's gratitude fanned out.

"I would like to invite you to lunch now, Clarabelle. Where shall it be?"

191

"Thank you very much. I usually go to a little place right across the street, the St. Louisian."

At their small table Clarabelle removed her glasses to polish them, giving her face rather cruel exposure. It looked suddenly unmasked; the pale grayish eyes had a shortsighted peer, the bite across the bridge of her nose from the glasses giving the effect of a scar.

What a pity such a kind, nice-mannered girl should not be prettier! Virgie wondered if Carl Schlachter had followed up the meeting she had maneuvered for them at the Christmas party.

No sooner had they ordered womanish luncheons than Clarabelle cleared that up promptly. "Who do you think telephoned me last night after all this time since your party and dated me for a dance next Saturday night at the Elks Club?"

"I couldn't guess," said Virgie, guessing.

"Carl Schlachter. One nice fellow, I thought, and his mother one nice woman. I appre——" Clarabelle was going to add, "I appreciate his dating me," but caught herself up. "I happened to be free for Saturday night," she added.

Why need nice girls so often be plain girls? asked Virgie of herself.

With self-conscious hesitation Clarabelle continued, "Did you by any chance ask him to call me, Virgie?"

"Why no, Clarabelle. I've only seen him myself once or twice since that night. His mother is such a lovely neighbor to me."

"I'm glad. I wouldn't want him to do it out of—duty."

"Child, what an idea!"

"I felt that way the one time my brother brought someone home. It looked like expectations for his sister."

"If I was a fellow, I would be mighty glad if a girl like you would condescend to go on a date."

"I wish fellows felt that way."

"Well, those that don't just don't know a nice girl when they see one."

"Sometimes I think it is the 'nice girl' that is my trouble. It isn't enough."

"It will be for Mr. Right."

"I would have come over to see you after the dinner, but I guess you know, my father and Uncle Charley, as Anchutz puts it, have been sort of Mr. Oil and Mr. Water. We're the water, he always says. It's cheap."

"From what Charley tells me, your daddy certainly had his own ideas about what he wanted and didn't want. I always respect that in people."

"I wouldn't trade the way we are with Claudia or Brock. Mom always said we made our bed and, even if it's lumpy, we like to lie on it. Lucky that all of us are that way, isn't it?"

"I guess I'm a little that way too, not one to kick about the bed I have to lie in."

Virgie drew up with an involuntary laugh. "Excuse me, but it made me think of a story about a—a story I once told your Uncle Charley about an upper berth on a train, and I don't believe he's stopped laughing yet."

"Tell it to me; I like funny ones."

"Maybe I better not—honey."

"Did you ever get a thank-you note from us after the dinner?"

"It was a mighty nice one."

"We all helped to write it."

"Your Uncle Charley was mighty pleased too. A little thing like that can help bring a family together."

"You're the one who is doing that. Aunt Myra and Uncle John Henry came over to our house last week for the first time in years, and we all agreed you did it."

"Like I tell Charley, a family should be like a good ship, weather its storms and sail on in one piece."

"Have you a family?"

"A son by my first marriage. Grant remained in the down-under country after the war. He was part of the ship of me. It didn't stay in one piece."

"I hope you're part of our ship now," said Clarabelle impulsively.

Virgie colored. "That is the very nicest thing that has been said to me. I'll think of it when—if I'm feeling not-taken-in."

"Virgie, why are so many of us lonely? It isn't because I'm not popular or not married. It seems to me there is just a lonely kind of desert way down inside everybody's life."

"I guess that's part of the scheme of our coming into the world alone and going out of it alone."

"I hadn't thought of it that way."

"But it's difficult, Clarabelle, for a woman to feel herself a whole woman if she doesn't marry."

"I want to be married! But you're married and lonely, Virgie."

"Don't misunderstand me. What you said to me a minute ago can rub out my loneliness. I've never been happier than now. I always say, 'Charley, you have moved me over into

Heaven Street.' Like you say, the loneliness is something separate, on account of being brought into a family that I don't really fit into. But I'm going to."

"You do. You do."

"You know, Clarabelle, here's a funny thing. No matter how happy one may be to live on Heaven Street, there are times when you miss something you've been used to all your life. Even the bad times, and I've had plenty. But now nobody in trouble or sick or poor comes to me any more. I'm glad of course that nobody is any of those things here—but you know what I mean?"

"I wish I didn't have to get back to the office! Don't forget, we're going to have a party at our house next. And, Virgie, sure you didn't tell Carl Schlachter to date me? He did it on his own?"

"He did it on his own."

Chapter 34

WARM STOVE

One afternoon when Charley was in St. Louis, Brock knocked on the door to Virgie's bedroom, where she was lying across the bed, reading the St. Louis *Post-Dispatch*.

"May I come in?"

She started to rise.

"Don't get up. I saw Dad leave the house without you and that happens so seldom, I thought you might be lonesome," he said with what was either a smile or a grimace.

"Your father has gone to the city on business that has to do with the memorial. That's going to be a mighty fine thing, Brock."

"Best thing he ever did, if for no other reason than to keep his two offspring from laying hands on more dough than they already have."

"It's a mighty fine tribute to your—mother."

He looked handsome as he sat at the foot of the bed, his light-colored hair damp as if he had perspired, his face, with its straight planes and good bone structure, bothered.

"What's on your mind, Brock?"

"I don't know," he said with an uncertain laugh. "Darned if I know."

"Now what kind of a way is that to talk!"

He began looking around the room in a disturbed way. She swung to the side of the bed, actually to get a whiff of his breath. Nothing.

"Can I sit here a while, Virgie?"

Now she had it! He was fighting off desire for it and had come to her.

She had once known a "sneak" drinker, a huge rough fellow, foreman of a wrecking crew, who used to show up occasionally on Pine Street with that: "Can I stay here a while, Virgie?"

"I'm crazy wild for a swig or two tonight, Virgie. Burning up, but I 'dassn't.' If I can get through tonight—Jesus, if I can get through tonight—can I stay here, Virgie, until my old man gets back?"

"How about a game of canasta?"

"I'd rather just sit here."

"Oh, let's go downstairs and have a try at it."

She brewed him coffee which he did not drink and as they played he kept rubbing his head.

"Headache?"

"No," he said and gave that seeking look around the room. What ailed this boy? She dared not probe.

She told jokes out of the rather noxious store of them she had come by through the years. One about a large black bull and a dainty friend, another concerning the immemorial traveling salesman who entered the immemorial wrong hotel

197

room—and Brock threw back his head for the kind of guffaws they elicited.

She told a third of similar vintage, but now, suddenly, he did not seem to hear, continuing to glance about, as if following a movement in the room.

They were still at canasta when Charley returned, in high spirits. "The Sprague Memorial is going to be the greatest of its kind in this state," he announced, rubbing his palms together and drawing a chair up to the card table. "Three of the architects went over every inch of the site with me today, and the location can't be beat. Wait till you see the blueprints they are coming up with this week. Room for a third? Deal me a hand. I need to calm down . . ."

Once or twice as the game wore on, Charley gazed at his son's suddenly somnolent face with a gathering lowering frown.

What the devil! What goes? Drink must be the answer to whatever it was. Yet nothing in his room except the untouched bottles; neither did he come home full of the stuff. What the devil!

His children were just so much failure. Settle for what you've got, and be glad it is no worse. Periodically this synthetic philosophy lasted for just so long and then began to wear thin.

But glancing now at Brock's white and purposeless-looking hands taking up the cards as loosely as he seemed to lay hold of everything else in life, old rages rumbled through Charley, but he pressed them down.

Damnation, even those dunderheads of Ed's had it over his own. No problems with them. Anchutz—chip off the old block; the girl—not much to look at, but feet on the ground. Why the devil did it have to be his girl, his boy, who kept missing and missing? Polly, of course, would have done a better job, but how much better? Didn't his kids have the stuff?

When he fell into such contemplations life was a gray moor. Except for Virgie. What a woman!

Gradually it became not unusual for Brock to seek Virgie out in the scraps of moments when she might be alone. He began to watch from his window for his father to leave the house. But on those days when Brock's door remained closed and he refused so much as a tray, Virgie's apprehensions were as great as Charley's.

"Dad, go away. I want to be alone for a while, is that a crime?"

Charley would throw up his hands in a gesture of helplessness.

"Brock," Virgie would call through her transmitter, the keyhole, "your father and I worry when you won't let us bring you something to eat."

"When I want to eat, I'll eat; don't you worry."

Then again a roar from Charley: "What the hell are you doing in there—boozing in solitary——"

"If it will make you feel better, no. Just demanding a little privacy, and, by God, I intend to have it. For God's sake, let me alone until I'm—ready not to be alone."

"Come away, Charley"—this in a whisper from Virgie—"some people are that way. Come times when they just have to be alone. I knew a woman like that once."

Charley beat against his forehead. "I want to help him. He's my son, damn it, and I—I—he's my son. Brock, what ails you in there—can't you tell your old man? Are you sick, boy? Is it drink or dope, son——"

"I've told you until I'm deaf, dumb, and blind. I—just need to be alone, for God's sake, let me be that—I came back here thinking I could be that—Virgie, take him away——"

"Come, Charley, Brock will be all right tomorrow—you'll see——"

The lengthiest of these retreats lasted about three days, after which, Brock reappeared precisely as if nothing had happened, somehow commanding by his bearing that everyone concerned behave in like manner.

But alone with Virgie, Charley worried away at surmises.

"Could the boy be going the way of his mother, Virgie? I'd rather see him dead."

"Don't think such thoughts, Charley! Even doctors don't agree that such things can be inherited."

"I guess I'm nuts about that boy or it couldn't do this to me."

"I don't pretend to understand it either, Charley. The boy isn't drinking in solitary, I could swear to that."

"Says you," replied Charley, running his fingers through his sparse hair. "And he's not a boy. He's a man who's never behaved like one."

"Men are slow to mature, Charley."

"I wasn't. Maybe if he had his living to earn he wouldn't be. I've messed things up, might as well face it. I don't know which is the worse, his coming home this way or the days when he lived at his club and I didn't know what was going on except that he was no good on the job. Something else is not normal, although I've no complaint on this score. He hates to part with a penny, no matter what his income."

"I can't figure it out either."

"His mother was that way. I never could get her to understand she didn't need to be saving. You're not much of a spender yourself, baby."

"I've got you, Charley—what more can I want?"

"No wonder Brock sticks around you as if you were a warm stove."

Chapter 35

THE GAL I MARRIED

ONE EVENING WHILE "THE CHARLEYS," AS ED ALWAYS RE-ferred to them, were seated in the gun room, watching a television Western, the telephone in the room adjoining rang and Virgie went to answer it. When she returned she turned off the set abruptly.

"What the heck, Virgie! I want to see if the city slicker gets her."

"You'll never guess who that was calling me. Claudia."

"I'll be darned. What did she want?"

"She says after the nice time she had the night of our dinner, she wants to know me better."

"She does, does she?"

"Invited me to have lunch with her at the Chase Hotel next Tuesday. For a 'gab fest,' she called it, between us girls."

"Put some horse sense in her head, Virgie. She's slipped

the halter and can't seem to get back in. She must have something special on her mind."

"I told her we haven't been anywhere without each other since we were married."

"What did she say to that?"

"That's when she said about the gab fest between us girls."

"What did you say?"

"That I would call her back. After all, you are her father. We should be asked together."

"Lord, you don't know children these days. She's not slighting me. She's just thinking of Claudia. You go right along. She's just discovered the kind of girl I married."

"Charley, I love to have you say that word. *Married*."

"The gal I married. The gal I married. Only I'm warning the gal I married not to make any dates until you ask Papa." He pinched her cheek. "I want you to go on not feeling right without me. Now telephone her you will meet her for lunch."

"I've never been in the Chase Hotel."

"Your old man don't take you places. Darn shame. You make it too nice at home."

Claudia, over a first martini, was already waiting at a secluded table in the large dining room when Virgie arrived in a very blue suit that matched her very blue eyes.

Claudia's elegance of dark mink, expensively simple sheath of a dress, small emerald clips, and mere dot of a hat gave Virgie a squirm which she could neither have analyzed nor put into words. Claudia could have.

What a mess of a pretty woman! moved through her mind.

From all her father had let out concerning her, and from

all she had been able to ascertain, she might easily have been one. Someone should take her in hand—dress her——

Regarding Claudia's unhappy face and struck by the resemblance between brother and sister— How tragic, mused Virgie, that both Claudia and her brother seemed to be missing whatever it was they needed or desired.

From what Charley and Brock had already revealed, Virgie anticipated what lay so heavily on Claudia's mind and in her expression. And yet they were still strangers, scarcely exchanging more than the amenities. To be sure, at the dinner party Claudia had almost tearfully revealed to Virgie, in the presence of her young escort, the self-imposed tragedy of her divorce. But then she had been heady with good wine.

Now she came right out with it. "Virgie, I need you."

"I kind of need to be needed."

"If I've been sort of standoffish, I think it was more the way my father did it than anything else. Not that he owed Brock or me an explanation; heavens knows we haven't bothered too much to give him any about ourselves."

"Your father may have his shortcomings, but he is a good man."

"I know. But whatever else he is, he hasn't much talent for fatherhood."

"He realizes that."

"Have you ever seen him in a temper, Virgie?"

"No, but I understand he has one. A whopper. He told me so."

"Well, don't ever. But it wouldn't be fair to bring you here to talk about that, yet it all leads up to me and my problem."

A waiter brought Claudia's third martini. They ordered lunch.

"Virgie, I married a big-league professional baseball player. One of the greatest. But there was one great difficulty. He was too good for me."

"Your father thought highly of him."

"He didn't at first. A baseball player didn't rate with him. We eloped. Frank wanted to wait and win him over. But I didn't want to run the risk of letting him see my father with his dander up."

"Your dad's dander, as you put it, couldn't be that bad."

"Says you. I hope you'll never see it. They say my mother did. But you must be a tranquilizer in disguise if you haven't seen it."

"Brock eloped too, didn't he?"

"And how! We're not prize chickens. But I wonder if you realize, Virgie, what our home lives have been. Brock once said our father hired everything in the world for us, servants, governesses, housekeepers, and everything else that could be hired. But he couldn't hire love. He had it for us. But he kept it locked up in the vault of himself as if it were a security or his last will and testament."

"Charley realizes that now."

"But I'm not here to talk about such matters, Virgie. I know it's nerve to bring you here, considering my big stay-away. It's about Frank. I want him back. For the two years since we've been divorced, I've known my mistake was a terrible one. Help me get him back, Virgie."

"Me?"

"Ever since you opened up the family ice jam, I've had

the feeling maybe you could do something like that for Frank and me."

"Does he know how you feel?"

"Know! I've gone to him. I've even humiliated myself and gone to his parents. I was never so sure of anything as I now am that I can make him happy if he will only remarry me."

"Were you unfaithful, Claudia?"

"No."

"Was he?"

"No. If only he had been or done one single wrong thing that could justify me! I was in love with him even when I was making things worse between us. What finally split us was the way I made him feel small to himself. As if you could reduce him in size. He was big in every way, mind and body. I somehow got lost along the way."

"In the days when my world was full of troubled people, I used to think that most of us grow a black forest somewhere inside ourselves and get lost in it."

"That's what must have happened to me, Virgie. I got tangled about what mattered—most——"

"Where is Frank?"

"With his parents in South St. Louis."

"I understand he's out of baseball."

"Yes, after we married, he went with Timmon and Timmon, the architects. He retired from baseball at twenty thousand a year to take an apprenticeship job at a hundred a week. That part was fine with me. But when my father offered to take him into business, Frank held out for architecture. 'All right to that,' I said, and it would have been, except that he wanted us to live on that hundred a week."

"What was wrong about that?"

"Virgie, I have the most beautiful little house in the world. Dad gave it to us when we were married. A jewel case. But Frank had his heart set on our moving out of it into an apartment, one that—that——"

"He could afford?"

"Exactly. It did something to his self-respect, he insisted, to live on his wife's money, instead of within his earning capacity."

"Didn't you admire that, Claudia?"

"I didn't see the sense of it. Get out of a little house pretty enough to have had its picture in *America at Home?* One we could so easily afford to live in, out of the money I inherited from Grandpa and what Dad settled on me? I couldn't see the need of it. Why allow myself only what Frank could afford? It just didn't make sense."

"It did to him."

"Well, anyway, that's what broke us up. One thing after another like that. With him it was live strictly within what he earned, and he intended to earn more and more. And he *has* earned more and more. In three years, he's already in line for junior partner in one of the biggest firms in the Middle West. Oh, Virgie, why didn't God or Dad or you come along before I cracked up my life?"

"Your father tried to many a time, Claudia. He told me so."

"Yes, but Dad always came at us with do's and don'ts and temper. Besides, I guess nobody could have stopped me."

"But what can I do, child?"

"Go to him, Virgie. You have a way with you. Make it happen. Frank is still in love with me. I know he is. His mother told me my picture is in his drawer. But he's afraid of me. Doesn't believe I'll keep my word and live his way, in order for him to feel a man, and not a kept one."

"But until you respect him in that, you won't make a go of it."

"But I do now. That's what you've got to make him understand."

"I should think that you yourself could do that better than anyone else."

"I tell you I've tried. I've never told this to a soul, but, Virgie, I got down on my knees to Frank the last time I saw him. Literally. I would do it again if I thought it was any use. I want my marriage back so terribly. There are other men I could marry tomorrow. But I want Frank. Virgie, help me."

Tears moved down the smooth planes of her cheeks.

"Claudia, I don't like to admit this, but in many ways I am a fish out of water, since I—married your dad. My old life keeps rising up to hit me. I fitted in back there. Not that I'm unhappy with your father. He's a prince. But I'm just trying to tell you I'm not up to what you're asking."

"You are. You're a person one trusts. I know I haven't the right to ask, much less expect."

"No, no, it's not that, but——"

"Then go to Frank for me. He's home on Sundays, slaving away over that drawing board of his. I can't tell you what to say, but I'll be praying every moment you are with him. Will you, Virgie?"

"I'll have to talk it over first with your father."

"Dad's for me. He's already tried his hand at talking to Frank. You will go if he's willing?"

"Of course."

Chapter 36

WOMAN TALK

FOR SEVERAL DAYS PRIOR TO CHARLEY'S DEPARTURE FOR
Jefferson City on affairs pertaining to the memorial, Virgie
had been awaiting her moment to capture his attention on
the matter of Claudia.

For weeks he had been in protracted conferences with
the mayor, city commissioners, a committee of citizens, with
his brother John Henry, and even with Ed, who had volun-
tarily asked to sit in on the project bearing the family name.

This last seemed to hit Charley with impact. "Darnedest
thing, calls me up and comes right out with it. 'Charley,'
he says, 'I hope you're going to let me put my nickel's worth
into the Sprague Memorial.'"

"'Have it on me, Ed,' I said. 'I'll put you down for fifty
thousand and glad to do it.' He comes back at me the same
old stiff-necked way. 'No,' he says, 'two hundred and fifty
dollars from me on my own, and you'll have my check in
the morning mail.'"

"You can't help but admire that, Charley."

"Damn it, you can't. You didn't put him up to it by any chance, did you, Virgie?"

"You know I don't do things behind your back. Speaking of behind your back, there's something that Claudia asked me to do, at the lunch. I told her I couldn't agree unless I talked it over with you first."

"That girl is as mixed up as an omelet. There's no unscrambling her."

"Are you sure, Charley, that you understand the entire situation? Sometimes children seem farthest away from those closest to them."

"I'm sorry for the girl, but she brought her house down around her own ears. Frank is finished!"

"But Claudia insists he is still in love with her."

"Maybe he is, but what he gave me to understand was pretty plain. A man that has got his head out of a noose isn't going to stick it back in."

"A man can change."

"That may be. But Frank is a serious fellow who hasn't time for upsets. He quit twenty thousand a year to get somewhere in the work he's selected for himself. He turned me down to prove he hadn't married the boss's daughter for any other reason than the boss's daughter. Claudia didn't have the sense to recognize a wonderful fellow for a wonderful fellow."

"She claims she has learned through this bad experience."

"But the man doesn't want her back, Virgie. He just doesn't want her."

"When a man is still in love, the way Claudia claims he is,

comes a time when he quits thinking about things with his mind and starts to think with his heart."

"Woman talk. But go ahead. I'm not stopping you."

"Would you go with me, Charley, if I wait until you return from Jefferson City?"

"Not on your life. That fellow gave me one brush-off worthy of a diplomat. I don't like for you to lay yourself open to more of the same, unless you think you can patch things. I wouldn't put it past you. Now worry a little about your old man. I'd like to take you to Jefferson City with me, if I knew what you would do with yourself while I'm hustling."

"I'll be busy at home, Charley, doing things you haven't the patience for me to do when you're around. It will be the first time we've been separated. The days will seem weeks."

"Good! Miss me big, baby," he said, pressing her body close to him as she slid onto his lap.

She whispered something that must have been on the raffish side into his ear, biting the lobe, and he guffawed.

"If I'm not back for supper Monday next I'll be home Tuesday in time for breakfast."

"You couldn't have a grander mission than the memorial, Charley. Stay as long as you need to."

That night, long after Charley's snores had moved into their snarling rhythm, she lay awake. Accustomed as she was to accommodating easily, this idea of catching Claudia's husband unawares in order to induce him to re-enter a legally dissolved marriage kept her wakeful.

She wished Charley had not dropped off to sleep, so that they might continue discussion.

Had he any actual realization of the individual tragedies of his un- and maladjusted children? Was he as immune as he seemed? Or had he learned by way of their hapless mother to thrust anguished appraisals from him? Had he actually thought that the large financial settlements would solve the problem?

Poor Charley, how little he knew of his girl Claudia, youth and beauty still hers, but the debris she had made of her life all about her.

As she lay wide-eyed, she could hear in the room above, pacing the floor, Brock in the throes of who knew what mysterious tortures.

Occasionally the forbidden thought flashed through her that Brock might be coming to grips with the same destiny that had overtaken his mother. Charley had never referred to what must have been the terrible circumstances that preceded her commitment. But her neighbor, Carl Schlachter's mother, had let fall that one midnight Polly had been taken to a waiting ambulance, screaming vituperative nonsense.

What strange forces must be at work in that tormented fellow upstairs! Back and forth. Back and forth.

She rose and opened the bedroom door to listen. Back and forth.

Chapter 37

NO

VIRGIE RETURNED ONLY ONE OF THE TWO OUTFITS SHE HAD purchased on approval at Clarabelle's suggestion.

Keeping in mind the unobtrusive hat which she had seen on Clarabelle, she rigged herself up a small replica in dark blue velvet with a tailored-looking rosette of matching felt, which she thought somewhat resembled an old-fashioned penwiper. But the effect, if not her preference, was "genteel."

She had worn the new frock for Charley, waiting to greet him in the front hall when he entered the house. He had pinched her and remarked, "Get out of that dress, baby. Get into one of your wrapper things."

But nevertheless, the Sunday morning she set out for Frank Hagedorn's, newly outfitted in the hat and dress, she felt nice-looking and right.

Brock had offered to drive her. But while there was neither sight nor evidence of alcohol, he had been locked in his room for the several days of Charley's absence in Jefferson City,

over a longer period than she remembered. She was glad
Charley had not been at home to take note of it.

"I would rather go by bus, Brock. I only have to transfer
once. Don't forget, I'm used to traveling that way. You take
a nice long walk. The fresh spring air will do you good."

"Fresh air? What's that?" he asked with a wan attempt
at levity.

It was one of those premature, false-spring March days,
and the little lawns before homes in the nicely kept residen-
tial area in South St. Louis, where the Hagedorns lived, would
any day be ready for the turning of the softened earth and
the dropping of seed.

The Hagedorns lived in a red-brick bungalow with a slant-
ing roof of colored slate, and a circular mound of brown
earth on the front lawn, that would shortly bloom with set-
out tulips.

An elderly man in overcoat and a fedora hat pulled down
over his eyes, suggesting a convalescent sunning himself, was
seated on the front porch.

He nodded pleasantly as Virgie mounted the steps, and
indicated the front door. "Good morning. The missus is indoors, getting ready for church," he said without curiosity.
"Marcy," he called through the open door, "a lady to see
you!"

Almost immediately a stout figure, obviously and stiffly
attired for church, appeared at the door.

"Are you the lady from the rummage-sale committee?"

"No, I——"

"My mistake!" exclaimed Mrs. Hagedorn, in a slightly
German accent that matched her husband's. "We were ex-

pecting one of the ladies from the church to collect what we had to send to the thrift sale."

"I am Mrs. Charles Sprague."

Mrs. Hagedorn stopped, paled. "Come right in," she said peeling off her stiff kid gloves. "You've caught us just leaving for church, but do come in. Herman, you come in too."

"I won't detain you. It's really your son I've come to see."

"Of course, of course," continued Mrs. Hagedorn, still in fluster. "I'm glad to see you. Herman, this is Charley Sprague's new wife. Do sit."

With much dragging of chairs, the three were finally seated in the modestly furnished front room. Two photographs in ornate filigree gilt frames, one of them Claudia, the other presumably Frank, faced them from the mantelpiece.

"I understand your son is home Sunday mornings?"

"Yes, Frank is out in his studio over the garage, where he works away at his drawing board. Herman, call Frank."

"Will it be all right," asked Virgie, rising, "if I go out to where he is?"

"You would rather be by yourselves?" inquired Mr. Hagedorn courteously.

"I—I guess you know why I want to see him. Naturally it is kind of private."

Mrs. Hagedorn produced a freshly laundered handkerchief from her handbag into which she proceeded to weep softly. "What you have come here for, Mrs. Sprague, my husband and I want as much as you do. Not, Herman?"

"Yes, we think it is best that this trouble between Frank and Claudia be patched up. We are not divorcing kind of people."

"Claudia knows a little bit too late that there don't come many like our boy. We tried to talk him away from this marriage in the first place. A beautiful rich girl, a little spoiled, we figured, and an independent fellow like our boy didn't look right from the start."

"His mother and I knew how Frank had his heart set on getting out of pro baseball after he passed thirty. From a child, he wanted to be an architect. The baseball was just one of those accidents."

"We wanted it patched up. My husband and I believe now that Claudia is willing he should make his own terms. The boy will never have eyes for anyone else. He don't talk, but I know my son like a book. He loves that girl," she concluded in the tone of strange-are-the-ways-of-the-world.

Virgie stood embarrassed before the two troubled people. "I don't see what I can do, but Claudia seems to think that maybe I can talk him back to her."

"Mrs. Sprague, you will be a godsend if you can. We will go on our way to church and leave you alone with him. He won't talk much, but you talk to him, please."

"That is what I'm here for."

"There is not a day he don't stand for a little while in front of her picture on the mantelpiece, and there is another he keeps hidden in his room."

"They got on badly only because she couldn't understand that a man like our son wants to be a man in his own home, even if it's not so fine as his woman could afford. Maybe you will call this false pride, but his mother and I can't help feeling good that he is that way."

"He overdoes it a little, maybe——"

Virgie nodded silently, feeling closed up with what she could not say.

"We will be praying in church while you talk to our boy. Can I fix you a cup of coffee before we go?"

"No, no. Do you think he will talk to me at all? So many of the family have already been here."

"He will talk to anyone who will talk about her. Show Mrs. Sprague the way to the garage, Herman."

And, God, show me the way, thought Virgie as she followed him.

As she faced Frank in the large bare room over the garage where he was working before a drawing board, Virgie thought, What a man, even better than the photograph had conveyed. Poor Claudia, sitting in her lonely house amidst the ashes of her mistake, the trees in her garden laden with Dead Sea fruit! It was to this man she had denied children and the right to his pride.

He seemed surprised when he identified herself. She had wanted to introduce herself as Claudia's stepmother, but the words clogged.

There were two wooden chairs in the room; he offered her one, and straddled the other.

"You can guess why I am here. I suppose I am the only one who hasn't been here." She wanted to say, "member of the family," but again the words clogged.

He nodded and waited.

"I don't know why Claudia chose me to come this time. I am no talker."

"That's all right; neither am I," he said, his smile filled with large white teeth.

217

"Claudia is young and beautiful; you are so young and handsome. Your lives should be that way too."

"That's what we thought they were going to be."

"They can still be, can't they?"

"I hope hers will be. I intend to try to make mine that way. I am an architect, and architects build. I intend to build a life."

"Don't architects ever tear up their plans for a house and start over again?"

"I'll say they do."

"And the second one is sometimes the right one?"

"Could be."

"You and Claudia could build from a second blueprint."

"Caught me that time unawares, didn't you?" He smiled broadly. "Not a bad simile or metaphor, was it, that you put over on me? Which would you call it?"

"I never heard of either."

"When I became a baseball pro my education flew out of the window. I am trying to get some of it back."

"Claudia is trying to get you back."

"Let me set you right. Good of you to come here. Good of all of you. I don't pretend that I've got her out of my hair yet. Maybe I never will. But I will never be any woman's paid gigolo. I'm out of that noose and I intend to stay out."

"A young man like you could never be that—a gigolo."

"Exactly."

"But being a hard man is the hard way to be a happy man. Your girl has softened up. She even told me to explain something to you that no girl should ever feel called upon to ask someone else to do for her."

"Then I wouldn't, if I were you."

"I promised her I would. Claudia says she had thrown away all her pride coming to you again and again and trying to undo what she has done to your lives."

"I don't intend to let it continue to spoil mine."

"If you still care for one another, it means spoiled lives in spite of yourselves."

He rose and walked to the small dormer window of the attic-shaped room and stood looking out toward the rear of his parents' house.

She continued as if he had not left his chair.

"Claudia not only wants me to say that she is glad now you gave up big-pay baseball, and expects to live on the income from your architect's position. She wants it that way."

"She thinks she does."

"And, Frank, here comes the private part. She wants a baby—babies, she said. And to tell you not just because you do, but because she does."

He turned. "You believe that?" he asked in a double tone of inquiry and challenge. "You believe that?"

"I do."

"You actually do. If only I could believe that. I want to believe it. Do I dare?"

She rose, taking up her handbag.

"Do I appear like a person who is lying to you?" she asked, staring into him.

"No."

Chapter 38

QUICKSAND

Lying alone in bed for the first time since her "marriage" could be a little frightening. For almost the entire week since Charley's departure for Jefferson City, Brock had scarcely emerged from his room. The pacing back and forth up there had become as ominous as the distant beating of war drums.

Sometimes, to shut out the sound, Virgie dug into her pillow, mashing it against her ears.

Once or twice she had tiptoed upstairs and stood outside Brock's door, listening. No sounds except the pacing. She would have given much to turn the knob and enter. But something larger than uneasiness deterred her.

The night before Charley's scheduled return, racked by the trochaic rhythm of the footsteps, she rose and, opening her bedroom door, clicked on the hall light, so that a patch of it came in and relieved the blackness. Then she lay down again, and dozed off.

When she awoke, not sure whether it was ten minutes or hours later, Brock in dressing gown, was standing in the open doorway. He was breathing with such heaviness that she realized it was these sounds she had been hearing through her sleep.

As she sprang from bed he laid his forefinger across his lips. "Don't wake the old man," he said in a coarse whisper.

"He's not here, Brock. Don't you remember? He's in Jefferson City for the week. We drove him to the station. Remember? He won't be home until tomorrow."

He slapped his forehead. "God, yes! I don't remember things."

She drew him toward her by the lapels of his dressing gown, seeking once more for a clue off his breath.

"Have you been drinking, Brock?"

"Wish to God I had," he said, leaning against the doorframe in weariness.

She led him into the room. "Then what is it?"

He sat on the side of the bed and dropped his face into his hands. "I can't go on this way any longer, Virgie."

She grasped one of his sleeves and pushed it above the elbow, revealing bare smooth arm; then the other sleeve.

"Wrong. Never a shot or a whiff in my life," he said with dreariness in his laugh and dug his head against her as she stood beside the bed. "Virgie, for God's sake," he cried, kneeling and clasping her knees, "help me to be man enough to end it! I can't go on!"

She sat down on the edge of the bed and drew him clumsily onto her lap as if he were an oversized child. "Tell Virgie quietly, Brock. Don't make those terrible sounds. The maids will hear."

"It's my third tonight. I can't walk them off any more."

"Your third what?"

"Fright. They come on me. I thought maybe if I came home I could stand it better. But it isn't that way. I can't struggle it alone any more."

"You're not alone, Brock. I'm here."

"Virgie, did you ever feel yourself begin to yell inside yourself, only you're yelling without a voice, and you open your mouth to let it out and nothing comes, and that frightens you until you sweat cold. Did you ever——"

"I don't believe so. Maybe you have nightmares."

"Oh, God, if I could only wake up and find they were! Did you ever see yourself coming toward yourself, Virgie? Did you ever feel someone following every step you take, and you want to run but for the life of you you can't because your legs are paralyzed and you can only keep doing that terrible inside yell that has no voice? Ever been through that, Virgie?"

The sound of his pacing, the memory of his explosion Christmas week, moved through her mind.

"It's not right that you should happen to be the one who has to hear all this, Virgie, but—somehow—you are. Why?"

"Because that's the way it has always been with me."

He fell back on the bed, racked with chill. "Hold me so I don't rattle my bones——"

She threw herself beside him, pressing him close for the warmth she could give him, drawing up the blanket.

"I'll call a doctor."

"No. There's nothing he can do for my kind of sickness."

"What kind?" she asked with dread.

Now he spoke with a strange, contemplative softness. "I'm

losing my mind, Virgie. For all the time they've been saying I'm a solitary souse, I've been losing my mind. Isn't that terrible?"

She pressed his face so tightly to her chest that his lips were closed and only mumble continued.

"Sh-h, you don't know what you are saying, Brock."

"I'm saying what I am," he whispered, jerking back from her. "I'm not a solitary drinker any more than you are. I'm a solitary lunatic. I'm losing my mind, like my mother before me."

"Your father will——"

"If you say one word of this to him, I'll shoot myself. There's time for him to know when there's nothing left but for him to know. It's easy for me to shoot——"

She slammed the palm of her hand resoundingly across his cheek. "Now will you come out of it?"

He dug down against her again. "Shock treatment won't help. I've slapped myself, beaten myself, when my head fell off my shoulders or the yelling began. Dad never let us go to see my mother. But she's before me all the time, except when I can't remember. Virgie, do you ever forget where or who you are? Sometimes I can't find me. God help me, I can't find me."

It required her full strength to hold down his noisy incoherence and restrain his vehemence by pressing the palm of her hand tightly against his mouth. When he finally subsided of exhaustion, she continued to lie quietly beside him, her one arm numb and aching, but still holding him close for reassurance.

While she daubed one-handed with the corner of the sheet

at the returning dampness of his brow, creeping drowsiness slowed his speech.

"You'll never tell my dad, promise me, Virgie. It will help me fight the fight to keep him from knowing."

"I promise, Brock."

"He's had the monkey on his back of twenty years of her madness."

"Sh-h-h——"

"Never tell or he'll have to send me away too. I'll kill myself first."

"I've promised you, Brock."

He seemed to sleep, but she dared not withdraw her hurting arm. Time dragged on. Her thoughts raced; her dreads raced. Could this be heritage? The facts that Charley had related to her seemed to say no, in a no-yes sort of way. Could Brock be suffering nothing more than what they termed a nervous breakdown, induced by fear? Could he lick it? People did. Psychiatrists did. Could Brock, if he would?

Despite the ache of holding him quiescent in her arms, she must have dozed.

She awoke to lights on and Charley standing in the sudden glare, his face terrible as Lear's!

Simultaneously and instantaneously the two of them were out of bed, on their feet, Brock in full possession of himself, Virgie, her negligee dragged back, standing in her flimsy nightgown.

"Charley, we didn't expect you until tomorrow. We didn't expect you!" What was she saying? Why was she saying it that way? Why was she afraid?

"Get out! Get out, or I'll kick you out!"

"Dad, for God's sake, you don't understand."

"Goddamn it, get her out before I let go of myself!"

"By God, you're going to listen or——"

"Get her out!"

"Brock—please—please—go. Let me talk to your father. Please——" she cried and shoved him beyond the door, slamming and locking it.

On the slam, Charley began a cyclonic rush around the room, flinging open closet doors, throwing shoes, hats, boxes, dresses, coats to the floor in the extremity of a man bereft of everything except massive rage.

"Go, goddamn, go! Before I throw you."

"Charley, let me——"

"Don't touch me! You're filthy!"

Now he began to drag down suitcases from the closet shelves, slamming them to the floor, and from the open drawers, flinging out contents, the box containing her few jewels opening and scattering its brooch, necklaces, and rings.

"Take your goddamn loot. Pack yourself out of here."

She fell on her knees. "Charley, see, I'm on my knees to you. It isn't what it seems. Just listen . . ."

"Out of here! I don't need to listen. I've seen!"

"Charley, you don't know what you're doing. Once I go . . ."

"Don't make me choke you!" he screamed. "Go where you came from, whore!"

She rose to her feet, arm across her face as if he had struck her physically, and began willy-nilly to cram some of the strewn clothing into one of the suitcases, kicking aside the box of spilled jewelry, sliding into a long coat over her nightdress. Hat tucked under one arm, hair flowing, she walked mechanically out of the room, down the stairs.

Over the balustrade, as she descended, Charley began throwing the remainder of the clothing into the lower hall, tossing after it two suitcases, and finally her handbag, into which he crammed a wad of folding money. "This is to pay you to keep out of my sight, and there will be a check for severance pay."

"I'll never cash it!" she cried back, tossing the packet of his bills to the floor.

"As you goddamn please. Go sleep with the next one's son."

She looked up tearlessly. "There will be no coming back. You know that, don't you, Charley?"

"Get the hell out!" he shouted and rushed back into the bedroom, slamming the door until the house rattled.

Suddenly Brock appeared in the lower hallway through a swinging door that led to the rear of the house. He wore a topcoat.

"Let him blow it out, Virgie," he whispered, his face smeared with pallor. "Sometimes the elephant forgets. Maybe he'll come to his senses."

"Maybe I have already, Brock. 'Whore' did it."

"Virgie, he's only raving crazy at what he thinks he saw."

"I know that. What he saw, he saw, but down underneath everything, he had that word ready."

"You remember, Virgie, I told you how the old man goes stark raving crazy in a temper."

"No, Brock. Deep down inside Charley, even though he didn't realize it until tonight, I've been whore to him from the start. Nothing can change that. Promise me you won't ever tell him what actually happened. He will never believe it. Don't let him turn against you, almost all he has left."

"Oh my God, what have I done to you!"

"Only what was bound to come sooner or later. I see that now."

"What have I done——"

"Go up to bed, Brock. And promise me you will live up to your determination not to tell him your ridiculous fears. He can't take much more. And remember, there is no coming back for me, no matter what. Work with your dad, Brock, and for him."

"I can't let you walk out at this time of night. I'll take you to a hotel."

"No."

"Take the cash, Virgie," he said, stooping for the scattered bills. "Pride won't pay your way."

"I've enough on my own."

"Then I'll drive you where you want to go," he said, slipping the roll furtively into one of her flung coats which he carried on his arm.

"I want to go where I used to live, on Pine Street."

"At this hour?"

"My landlady lives in the building. She will find a place for me overnight. Maybe my old flat is vacant. It has been on and off since I left."

"I'll drive you there."

His tears ran as he drove, and she kept wiping them away with her handkerchief. "Stop it or we'll have to turn on the windshield wipers," she said, trying to be facetious.

"A stone would cry at what I've done to you."

"Brock, would it surprise you if I said maybe it is all for the best? I never realized until tonight that this whole business was on quicksand."

"What goddamn good has my life been to anyone?"

"Don't say that. Your future is not behind you. Fear is all that ails you. Who was it—Shakespeare? he seems to have said everything, or was it Roosevelt?—who said we have nothing to fear but fear. But anyway, you don't have to step outside of yourself, Brock, for your cure. Will you remember what old Virgie is saying to you these last minutes? Fear is what ails you. Lick it."

"I need you, Virgie; I needed you before I ever laid eyes on you. For God's sake, don't walk out on me too." He drew the car up so sharply beside a curb that a passing motorist, veering to avoid collision, hurled an epithet.

"Virgie, whatever is to be between you and my father, don't desert this rat on the sinking ship of himself."

"You're not a rat on a sinking ship, and even if you were, a rat jumps for his life. With or without me, you will never survive so long as you think wrong."

"Maybe it is just as well."

"That is for you to decide, Brock. Because at this rate tomorrow, even tonight, your ship may sink. It's too good a ship to have it happen."

"And you won't raise a hand?"

"If I thought it would help, I would keep it raised for you. If my thoughts of and for you, wherever I may be, will help, I promise them to you day and night."

"You mean long-distance."

"I'll pray for you too, Brock. Never could bring myself to talk about such things. But if it will help you to know, I pray a good deal. I'll pray and pray."

"Virgie, don't leave us."

"I won't in spirit."

"Stay in the flesh. My dad will come to his senses."

"Never, after the terribleness of what he thinks happened between you, his son, and me. Help him to know that it is better this way. I need to be what I am, or I don't exist for anyone, including myself."

"Then you're finished with us."

"Get back to your normal self, Brock. Build a life. You and your dad are two men alone. Merge your lives."

"Then this is actually final."

"As final as death. I guess you know your father and I are not married in the eyes of the church or state."

He stared into a silence that lengthened. "But Dad will make a money settlement."

"I have enough on my own. Now drive me, Brock."

They continued their ride to lower Pine, along the almost deserted streets.

"I'll run up ahead and make sure that Gram is there. Her rooms are just above the grocery store; my old flat is over hers. Put my bags out on the sidewalk. You mustn't come up."

"This is good-by, then? Down here on the sidewalk at one o'clock in the morning?"

"Definite and final, Brock. Be good to your father, and remember, all you need to cure yourself of is fear. God bless and help you."

He sat in the car and watched her climb the outside stairs.

Hat slapped willy-nilly on her head, she climbed. Presently a light popped on in a side window of the apartment into which Virgie disappeared.

Placing the suitcases on the sidewalk before the grocery-store window filled with canned fruit and boxed cereals, Brock re-entered his car, drove slowly away.

When he finally turned into the grounds of his father's house, Charley was sitting in the entrance hall, his hands dangling loosely, as if they had been boned, between his knees.

Apparently emptied of rage, weakness had hold of him. His mouth, although his teeth were still sound and firm in their gums, had suddenly that sunken look of a man with his dentures removed. He was an old man with red rims around his eyes.

"It's a terrible thing that happened here tonight, Brock. I went crazy. Sit down."

"Here in the hall?"

"I'm in the middle of a weak spell that hit me all of a sudden."

"I'll get you——"

"No, sit."

They sat side by side, staring into silence. A bronze Psyche on a newel post held a dim light over them.

"I know how it must have appeared to you tonight," began Brock, controlling his voice to match the deadly level of his father's, "but may God forgive you for the horrible mistake you made."

To his incredulity, Charley laid an affectionate hand on his son's knee, and his voice became sly and prideful.

"She may have picked your old man for a sucker, but just the same, the ones I pick are good enough for the young one too. Shows I can still compete with them. There's still life in these here bones, isn't there?" he said and nudged.

Oh my God, said Brock into his palms, the knee beneath his father's hand twitching.

"A good-looking number while she lasted. She had me fooled. And how."

"Dad, let me——"

"It's all right, son. I had her. You had her——"

Brock made a sudden lunging gesture toward his father and sank back trembling.

"I should have smelled the rat if I had taken the trouble to sniff," continued Charley. "Come to think about it, I did sniff in the beginning, but not enough. But no harm done, except a lot of cover-up and explaining to do. No fool like an old fool, eh, son?" The insinuating hand went down again onto Brock's knee and he rose to rid himself of it. "But not such a fool as you might think, eh, Brock? The marriage license is written in invisible ink on invisible paper."

"I wish to God I were back in the Army. I'd rather be in on a killing—than this."

Then Charley also rose, strength flowing back, and slapped his son whackingly between the shoulders.

"It's all right, boy. We're going out on the town together. I'll help you keep off the bottle and you'll help your old man keep young. There is still plenty of life left in him."

"I—I—goddamn it, I made a promise, but you don't know what you're talking about. Virgie and I——"

A flare of rage came back into Charley's voice. "Shut up! Never let me hear that name. A woman who would take a man's son to bed with her is a whore through and through."

"If you weren't my father, I could hit you for that."

"I say it again and again. I saw what I saw. She's dirty and, God forgive me, I liked her—I liked her so much——"

He stumbled his way up the stairs, to the sound of sobs that had no tears in them.

Chapter 39

SHE HAD BEEN CRYING
IN HER SLEEP

REVEREND POLKINHORNE LAY SLEEPLESS. FOR WEEKS that had become months he had been awakening, almost to the moment, at three o'clock in the morning.

The bedroom he shared with Blossom in the renovated rectory was never quite dark. A blue night light diluted it, and on moonlight nights such as this, one could have read large print.

Before the birth of the twins the curtains had been drawn against this night whiteness. But now the Reverend could see the two babies in their double crib across the room. At their feeding time, if one or both cried or needed changing, he could be on his feet in a flash, walking one or both of them, spanking them softly back to sleep with a sedative rhythm, or heating their formula in the improvised kitchenette set up in a clothes closet.

Through the cryings and the heatings Blossom slept softly, her fair hair about her shoulders. Her characteristic attitude—

233

one arm outflung, palm upward—was especially lovely to the Reverend. Sometimes as she lay, like Ophelia, he stood regarding her, a babe in each of his arms.

Often nowadays, unprecedented in his experience, the Reverend dozed off at his desk for want of sufficient sleep. A man given to intensive prayer he now, during these sleep-riddled nights, spent longer periods than ever on his knees. Always assuming the suppliant attitude in prayer, he would ease himself noiselessly from beside Blossom to the floor.

Almighty One, grant me the power and wisdom to bring contentment to this home. Endow the wife, the mother of our children, with whom Thou hast blessed me, with peace of spirit. Help her to ease her troubled mind and find her way closer to You. Help her through the confusions of youth, and the worship of false gods, into the light of Thy countenance, so that it may shine into her soul and light her way. Give me strength that I may succeed where I have fallen short. Bless our dear children and those that we pray are yet to come. Bless their dear mother and guide us through the fog . . .

The wail of a child cut through the silence of this particular moonlit night and into the Reverend's suppliance. Knowing the separate voices of his infants, he sprang to the proper side of the crib, diapered with precision, and drew the covers more snugly around the second child.

Moonlight strewn all over her, Blossom slept undisturbed. He stood beside the bed, looking down at her in the act of sleep, his senses as always stirring. And now he noted, as he had several times before of late, that there were wet paths down her cheeks. She had been crying in her sleep! The fright that frequently overlaid him took hold again.

What was eating into the soul of his unhappy girl?

Actually he knew, but forced back the awareness. A woman dissatisfied with her bargain. A wife cast in an incompatible role. A child who needed to be a woman but could not find her way.

Had everything been a mistake? A man of the cloth needed to choose a mate fitted by temperament to meet the requirements of his calling. But he had wanted her as wife, and as minister's wife, yet somehow the two were not coinciding.

How like a flower she lay there! The sight of the wet cheeks crowded tears into his throat. Her white breasts, so beautiful when her babies lay against them! Oh my dear, he cried within himself as he regarded her, you are not failing me as my woman; do not fail me as my wife and mother of my children.

The moonlight receded and dawn began. In another two hours it would be time to awaken her with a breakfast tray which he would prepare, a labor of love that made it effortless.

The buses which the Ladies Auxiliary of Rock Church had chartered to convey all fifty of them to the St. Louis levee, there to board a steamboat for the all-day round trip on the Mississippi River, would be leaving West Grove at ten.

As the minister's wife, Blossom was exempt from producing any share of the picnic luncheon. But cards for bingo, canasta, and bridge, candies, nuts, baseballs, bats, and souvenirs would be expected of her out of the bazaar fund in her keeping. The Reverend had purchased them and assembled them in the lower hall the night before. Blossom's mother, who was to take over the babies, would arrive at eight. His own appointment with a visiting bishop was at nine-thirty.

For want of sufficient sleep he suddenly felt almost unbearably fatigued. He longed to lie down beside his wife, luxuriate in the warmth of her nearness, and snatch what sleep he could. She was crying again, the tears seeping through her closed eyes, and as he regarded her she suddenly opened them, crying out, "No, no, no!"

"Darling," he said, "you are crying and talking in your sleep."

She sat up supporting herself with her arms stiff and palms flat on the bed. "Tell me it isn't true!"

"You've been dreaming, darling."

"Oh, you!" she said, fully awake now. "I was having a bad dream." Suddenly her eyes darkened and she clutched his arm. "Yes, yes, it is true. I want it to be a dream. I won't let it be true. I tell you I won't!"

"What, darling, what?"

"It's six weeks and not a sign, and I'm so regular. I'm pregnant! I should have gone to a doctor a week ago. I've been afraid. I can't face another. I won't."

"My darling," he said, scooping her in his arms. "My beautiful sleepy darling, you don't know what you're saying."

"Don't tell me I don't know what I'm saying! I haven't had twins for nothing. I know even before the doctor tells me. Phillip," she cried, grasping his jacket, "don't make me have more! Phillip, if you love me don't make me."

"My darling, my darling, God is touching us."

She beat against him with her small fists. "I don't want

Him to touch us, if it means going through it all again. Pray for me, pray for me not to."

He gripped her wrists. "God forgive you."

She looked into his anguished stare, her young face awry with despair. "What if I should die this time, Phil?"

"My poor sweet," he cried, softening, "my poor frightened sweetling. God is about to give a life to you." He lay down beside her and dried her cheeks with his lips. "My little love. God is kissing our lives. Of course you are a little nervous, but just look at our Rosamond and Cecilia over there in their cribs. They came so easily. You remember, almost before you realized it, they were in your arms——"

"It's too soon to have more. Too fast. We haven't had time to live yet ourselves."

"Blossom, you don't mean that. It's part of your nervousness. What is nobler living than creating a family? Lie quietly and go back to sleep, my darling, and remember, the buses leave at ten."

She sat upright at that. "The boat ride! The Ladies Auxiliary. The women, the women, the women. Another day. Another bazaar. Another strawberry festival. Another thrift sale. I can't take any more of them, Phillip."

"I know, darling, it gets a little monotonous."

"A little monotonous," she cried wildly, "a little monotonous! How under can understatement be!"

"We'll have to devise a way to relieve you of some of those duties. I've a few ideas. I sometimes feel the same way about too much of the same. It gets that way one way or another for most of us, darling."

"No, it doesn't. The other young-marrieds we know in and out of the congregation do young things. They can afford baby-sitters. What do we know of going to dances or into the city to shows? We are middle-aged while we are young. Phillip, life is passing us by."

"My dear, you don't know what you are saying. God is filling our cup until it runneth over."

"For you, perhaps. Not for me. And now since Dad got caught so bad in Wall Street, and can no longer help us, not even a part-time maid or anything beyond your salary and the few weddings and funerals——"

"Where have you lost the way, Blossom?" he asked in a kind of bewilderment.

"You should have married that What's-her-name Sprague girl with the buck teeth. Bazaars and bingo, strawberry festivals and cooky sales are just her meat. I'm wrong for you, Phillip," she cried, clasping her arms about his neck and kissing him. "I love you and our twins, but I don't want any more. I'm wrong for you."

Chapter 40

WHITE SATIN

Each time Myra arrived at the little house on School Street she was struck with recurring frequence by the fact that her mother, deep in her seventies, seemed to have shrunk a little more, not only in stature, but in face. Wrinkled as a prune, Myra could have covered it with her hand.

If she attempted to bolster her parent with good words about her appearance, the old lady waggled a gnarled forefinger.

"Don't *schmear* me. I look like an ugly old eagle with no feathers. Thank God your papa didn't live to see me so. It's bad enough you should."

The simile struck with force. Her mother did resemble an old ruin of an eagle, in no way suggesting the photograph of Yetta Moissevitch, the bride, which stood on the mantel.

Returning from a tour of recitals before ladies' clubs in Moberly, Salem, and Jefferson City, Missouri, Myra felt relieved that it was Friday, her evening on School Street. John

Henry would be having dinner with his brother Charley and possibly, she hoped, learn something of Virgie's mystifying absence.

In her strange beds in small-town hotels she had been dreaming of her mother in her tiny old house, the broken-down Topel and an unskilled Yiddish-speaking maid her sole bulwarks. What in case of fire or stroke? Her wisp of a mother, diminishing before her eyes, going closer and closer to the brink of death, her life as alien to her daughter's as if they dwelt on separate planets.

This time, however, when Myra arrived at the School Street house, Yetta, instead of her usual black cotton with white crocheted collar held by an oval brooch containing a photograph of a husband long deceased, was attired in her black silk, reserved for such rare occasions as a *bar mitzvah* or High Holidays.

Yetta had a faint pink flush on her cheeks, or could it have been a touch of rouge!

"Mama, you look like Rosh Hashanah."

"That's what I said," agreed Mr. Topel, who was already on hand for the Friday-evening ritual.

"I don't understand a married woman should run around the way you do, Myra. Concerts are not for wives."

"I'm seldom away from John Henry more than two or three days at a time, Mama."

"It's not that I ever see much of you, but at least it's a comfort, if I wake up in the night, maybe with a pain or my heart fast, to know if I've got to have you, I've got you."

"No matter where I am, you know you've got me," humored Myra. "You look wonderful, Mama."

"That's what I said," again agreed Mr. Topel.

"I wish you would dress up every night, Mama; it is good for your morale."

"For my what?"

"For your—spirits."

"That's what I said."

"You don't look so bad yourself, Topel. Sprucing up must be contagious. Isn't that a new suit?"

"It was my son Jacob's, may he rest in peace."

The candles already lighted flickered a faint design of movement over the white cloth, over the decanter of red wine and the *challah* covered with an embroidered linen square.

Tall silver candlesticks, Myra's recent gift, replaced the plated ones she had known through her childhood. Evening began to close in like darkening hills.

As far back into her childhood as she could remember, she had seen her mother cover her head with the white cap, raise her hands over the candles with a circular rhythm, and intone:

> *"Baruch atoh adonoy elohanu melach*
> *h'olem*
> *Asher kidoshonu b'mitzvohsov*
> *v'tsivonu*
> *Le had lik ner shel-Shabbes"*

The evening John Henry had attended these rituals with her Myra had asked her mother to read the prayer in its English translation.

"Blessed art Thou," intoned Yetta, the words not fitting her lips, "Lord our God, King of the Universe, Who hath sanctified us by His commandments, and commanded us to kindle the light for the Sabbath."

But tonight the words as the fathers spoke them came sweet as ripe figs to Yetta's lips.

From there on, the meal moved into normalcy, Yetta as always rejecting proffered aid, herself carrying to the table the steaming tureen of chicken stewed in its own juices and flanked with matzoth balls, the piled dishes of red cabbage, sweet-sour beets, and the bud of garlic which Topel liked to rub into his dinner plate.

"Why, Mama, those roses in the vase over there! You must have been to the five-and-dime store. They look almost real."

"They look almost real," repeated Yetta, clapping the palm of her hand across her mouth, her eyes, ancient as a monkey's, sparkling impishly. "Those roses *are* real, Myra. You tell her, Topel."

"*Ach*, Yetta, you tell her."

"I want it should come from you. It's a man's place to speak to the mother, and now that I am an old woman, Myra has become more my mother than she is my child."

He placed a shriveled hand that trembled across Yetta's.

"Go on, Topel. Myra won't bite. It is good news for her."

"Yetta and I want to get married."

Following the blurt of words, Myra sat, looking from one to the other, no words forthcoming.

"I wanted we should tell it to you together, Myra, so you wouldn't say nothing to me alone that you wouldn't say in front of Topel. It happened while you were away. It is settled."

"It is settled," repeated Topel.

"Go on, Topel, don't just repeat after me. Tell it exactly like I told you to tell. The way it happened. I am not ashamed."

"I am sitting here. Yetta is sitting there. It was last Monday night, wasn't it, Yetta?"

"He asks me what night it was! Suppose I wasn't here, who would you ask?"

"It was Monday. I am sitting here."

"You've already put yourself sitting there. Go on."

"It is Monday night, and I have come over after supper for checkers. I am sitting here, and it is her move, and all of a sudden she musses up the whole checkerboard."

"I did!"

"She musses it up."

"You said that once, Topel."

"And says to me——"

"Go on, Topel, and what did I say?"

"She says to me, 'Let's get married, Topel!'"

Yetta's hand was across her mouth again, her eyes filled with laughter. "I said, 'Let's get married, Topel,'" she repeated, her voice muffled by the hand and merriment. "All of a sudden it comes over me to say, Topel, let's get married."

"I think she is making monkeyshines, and I start to get the checkerboard back in order."

"I never was making less monkeyshines in my life," said Yetta with sudden sobriety.

"Then she gets up, comes around to me, like this, and—it should happen to me—kisses me on the neck and says——"

"Could I help it that it lands on the neck when he turns his face away?"

"I couldn't believe my eyes, so I turn them the other way, to see if they saw the same from the other side."

"And what did I say, Topel?"

"She says, 'To get married will be the most wonderful thing in the world for both of us.'"

"That's the way it happened, Myra. I am playing checkers——"

"We said that, Yetta."

"I am playing checkers, itchy the way I always am when he is so slow on his moves. When all of a sudden it comes over me, something I had never given a thought to before."

"I'm a little man, Myra."

"A *nebich*," interpolated Yetta fondly.

"A woman like your mother, as far up from me as the sun, comes at me. Naturally I think she is making fun."

"Surely you were, Mama."

"About such a thing like marriage, you don't make fun. All of a sudden it strikes me like lightning."

"You said that once, Yetta."

"Here I sit. Here both of us sit. As if we sit in a theater, waiting for the curtain to fall on our lives. Waiting for the end."

"No, no, Mama."

"No, no, she says, and, Yes, yes, I say. How many years is it we counted, Topel, you have been coming to this house?"

"Eighteen years and five months."

"And eighteen years, Myra, since you left me to marry a *goy*."

"Mama, I never left you."

"Ah, Myra, you married in this town, but you married

244

farther away from me than if your husband had taken you to live in China. Nineteen times in eighteen years he has set foot in this house. My eighteen birthdays, and one Pesach, besides."

"John Henry has always said, 'Get your mother anything she wants,' you know that."

"Did I say not? But why does he come? Because you say to him he should pay me respect on my birthday. But I don't hold it against him. What do we have to say to one another? Nothing. But me and Topel, we can talk for hours even if we have nothing to say."

"That's right, Myra. Your mother and I laugh, believe me, even when there is nothing to laugh about."

"And if we got to cry in the few years we have left, God forbid, we can cry together, not, Topel?"

"We can cry together. But Yetta and me have got good life left in us," replied Topel, and laughed as if there were springs in his chest.

"Topel has got his pension. I got the social security. Topel has got two thousand and two hundred dollars in the savings bank. I have got five thousand."

"And more brains than the two of us together," amended Topel.

"I like the *schlemmil* in you, Topel. Maybe you never did much in business, or much in life, but it kept you a sweet *schlemmil*. Not a big man, hard like a rock. Myra's father, *selig*, may he rest in peace, had ambitions. I always say it shortened his life."

"She likes me, a *schlemmil*, can you beat that?"

"What can I say to you two dear people? What can I say?

Why shouldn't you marry? And yet, and yet—why should you——"

Her glass of tea lukewarm, Myra closed her eyes, ashamed of what moved through her darknesses.

These two shriveled bodies, old trees, the sap no longer rising in them, and long since done with bearing leaves, lying side by side on their bed of mutual impotence.

"Mama, Mama—are you sure?"

"Yes, Myra."

"Then who am I to dare dictate?"

Who am I indeed? she thought into the darkness behind closed eyes. Had she not for eighteen years on end lain beside her man with mustered endurance, liking him, but bearing with his passion because it was his right? Who indeed was she, who had resisted him during his potent years for fear —yes, for fear of children by this stranger, John Henry.

"Mama, what you and Topel want, I want."

"Believe me, Myra, Topel and me together will be the best thing that could happen to you too."

"Not the way you mean, Mama."

"Like always you would be a good daughter. But when you walk out of this house Friday nights, what do I know of your life or your people? At my age, except for Topel and the few friends left who have not yet died off, and my sister in Israel who I have not seen for thirty years, I am more and more without my people. You know for how long your aunt writes we should come to Israel? Ten years. And now together we can go, not, Topel?"

"You mean to Israel?"

"Like me, Topel is homesick too for a place he has never seen."

"Yes, like Yetta, since Israel is here, I want to go back to where we began. I too have a cousin there who escaped from a German concentration camp after they killed her husband and children."

"We want to go where we would never have to feel the way we would if we should have to live with you in a *goische* world, no matter how good. We want to feel Israel under our feet. The Bible tells how our people walked there two thousand years ago."

"God bless you both, my dears, my dear dears."

"Topel wants we should have the wedding in the *shul*, like we were twenty."

"Of course."

"She should wear a white satin, Myra."

"Not for a widow, Topel. Mama should wear gray."

"He wants it white, all right. Who shall do us something if he wants it white?"

"Then white satin it shall be, Mama."

"You're not mad at me, Myra?"

"Mad? No, no, Mama!" she cried, suddenly glad. These two, almost grotesque with years, together as she would never know it—had never known it—were going home together.

So was she, but only to her kind and good stranger-husband with whom she shared no call of the blood. Mama should have her white satin, the marriage canopy, the weeping women, the orthodox wedding, tribal and traditional.

Someday, God and John Henry willing, she too might visit Israel, tread its cobblestones, the ancient blood and tears of her people dried into them, and face the immensity of

247

desert sands, the footprints of two thousand years of her driven forebears plowed deep under.

Darling, ridiculous pair, her mother and Topel, the common blood stream of their common heritage in full flow.

A white satin wedding gown for Mama!

Chapter 41

MR. HIMSELF

CLAUDIA'S BEDROOM WAS THE COLOR OF WHIPPED CREAM with a dash of chocolate in it. She had worked with painters, decorators, dyers, to achieve a tint she had carried in her mind as if it were a certain musical note.

She was like that, a perfectionist in the niceties. She was paying dearly for being like that.

Stretched on a chaise longue, hands locked behind her head, she lay, regarding space, a cream-colored telephone ringing insistently into it.

Three identical boudoir lamps lighted the modernistic scene of pale carpeting, upholstery, and window drapes, twin beds with tufted cream satin headboards.

A maid appeared in the doorway. "Do you want me to answer the telephone, Mrs. Hagedorn?"

"No, Patsy, let it ring. He'll get tired."

Patsy flared wider a cluster of white roses in their vase.

"If I had a Mr. Otis sending me these roses every day I would be answering the telephone, all right."

Claudia turned her head toward the wall. "Take them up to your room if you like them so much. I'm sick of the sight of him. I'm sick of the sight of them all."

"Moping isn't going to get your mister back, Mrs. Hage-dorn. It will only make you less pretty. What is to be, will be, I always say. Might as well have a good time, anyway."

"Where *is* the good time, Patsy, just tell me that."

"A lot of it is in the dark movie theaters for me with the boy friend. It may be for you in that there ringing telephone. Don't the ringing get on your nerves?"

"If it's Mr. Otis, he's due to stop about now."

"You may be missing something you was never meant to miss."

"You don't miss what you don't want."

"Someone is missing a lot, not seeing you lie there so pretty that way."

Claudia turned on her side and dug her face into the curve of her elbow.

"Wake me at six. Dinner at seven," she said, closing her eyes on Patsy and her ears to the ringing.

"Just the same," concluded Patsy doggedly, "that may be somebody else besides Mr. Otis. That may be Mr. Himself," she reiterated, tiptoeing from the room with the vase of roses.

Mr. Himself! The phrase hung after she had gone. Eyes still closed, Claudia reached toward the telephone, rested her hand with the narrow wedding band on the receiver, lifted it finally from its cradle.

"Hello. . . . Who? . . . Frank! I can't believe it!" Swinging to the side of the couch, she held the instrument close, as if for contact. "Frank, I've been lying here for hours, thinking, thinking—of you. . . . Yes, yes, I'll be home any time you say. . . . Right away? Where are you? . . . Then come for dinner at seven. I thought I was having it alone, and now I'm having it in heaven. Oh, thank you, darling, thank you. Whatever you want to see me about, good or bad, thank you for letting me hear your voice."

In a haste that made waste, she tore open drawers, tossing their orderliness into confusion, jerked dresses from their hangers to the floor, leaving them there as she sought out the one she had in mind, a slim, long-sleeved black with fluted white ruffles over her hands. He liked plainness.

Aware that the austere black, lighted by the rhinestone-studded net she had slipped over her blond hair, would not diminish her honey-colored beauty, she felt equipped to sustain the quiet composure she had determined upon.

Since their divorce Frank had never once responded to her emotional outbursts of regrets and entreaty. Whatever his mission, reserve might serve her better than tears.

She opened the door to him herself, greeting him lightly. "Hello, Frankie."

He entered on a whiff of warming spring evening, closed the door behind him, patted her forearm, and strode familiarly into the living room.

"What'll it be?" she asked with what casualness she could.

"As usual."

She poured him an inch of scotch whisky onto cubes of ice, another for herself, and, restraining her impulse to share the divan with him, seated herself opposite.

He rattled his ice and regarded her. "You look a million, Claudia."

"You look two million, Frankie."

They were still strangers talking patter across a distance. He had not, as she had crazily surmised he might, come to take her back. Whatever his reason, already it was evident they were to remain strangers.

He leaned forward, twirling his glass between his palms. She loved him in that characteristic attitude, his shoulders wide and strong, his head lowered.

"Claudia," he began, stirring his drink and watching the cubes whirl, "I guess you're wondering why I'm here."

"Yes, Frank."

"As a matter of fact, I'm almost as surprised as you must be."

"Could it be because you wanted to come?"

"A woman came to see me the other day, Claudia, your— I guess you would call her your stepmother."

"I had never thought of her that way, but I guess, yes."

"Well, anyway, you knew she came to see me."

"Yes, Frank, I asked her to."

"Where did your father find this—lady?"

"So far as we know, in St. Louis. They just came home one day, married. Beyond that, Dad has been about as receptive to questions as a clam."

"I must say that after the first shock of surprise, I liked her. But—well——"

"I know what you mean. So do we like her. That's why I'm surprised that what I felt was sure to happen should happen so soon."

"What?"

"It's ended. She's gone."

"Where?"

"Nobody knows that, either. Dad won't talk except to say he and Virgie have decided by mutual agreement to separate and it was for the best it's ended. If Brock knows anything beyond that, Dad must have clammed him up too."

"But it hasn't been much more than a week since she came down to see me."

"And I lunched with her just a couple of days before that. The whole family is stunned."

"Well, I'll be darned! Married and divorced practically the same year."

"Not exactly that. When I asked my father about divorce, he said that would not be necessary. There was nothing to undo."

"Well, I'll be darned. Just the same, there was one nice woman."

"She took something we needed away with her and she left something behind that we need."

"If the truth be told, that's why I'm here, Claudia. She said something on the corny side the day she came down to see me, but it stuck. 'Make sure,' she said, 'that while you are throwing away discarded things you don't want that you don't cast out precious things.'"

"Frankie," she said softly, "you are precious to me beyond anything on earth."

He caught her to him. "You are love and life to me," he said, kissing each word into her lips. "I can't live by will power any longer. I need to live by you and with you and for you."

"I've cried so for you, Frankie."

"Are you sure this time just what it will mean? Do the same things still matter most to you?"

"You matter most. That is what I have been trying to tell you over the dreadful months. Everything on your terms, Frankie."

"No, not on my terms. On our terms."

"Our terms."

"First I must bring you up to date on what has happened to me."

"It doesn't matter, Frankie, better or worse."

"But it does. Claudia, I want to try life for at least a few years in the new state. The forty-ninth."

"You mean Alaska?"

"Yes. Alaska is a new country, a new state, with new populations certain to flow in. I want to help create its new cities, its new homes, its new beauty."

"Frankie, how do you know——"

"I don't know. I believe. Alaska has no place to go but up. It will be like the little birth of a little nation. I intend it shall be the little birth of a big dream for me, or—for us."

"How big can you dream, Frankie?"

"It only seems that way to us, Claudia, because we are so small. We seem so tremendous to ourselves, when actually we are infinitesimal in the scheme of things."

"Pain isn't small—ever."

"Exactly. Just take your hot-and-bothered, good and bad, happy and suffering family. Each one is as big as the universe to himself. So are you. So am I. But actually we're all only tremendous trifles."

"No trifle, even a tremendous one, could hold all the suffering I have felt these months. There is no life for me except with you—wherever."

"Even if the whenever be now; the wherever, big, wide, and forty-ninth?"

"And the whoever, you!"

"Like it along with me, Claudia. Paul Krupps, a junior member of our firm, likes the idea well enough to go to the new state with me."

"With us."

"Bless you for that 'with us.' We'll probably go on ahead of him. There is always a chance that a dream may be full of holes. But my faith is in this one. My assured income should be about the same. Krupps is less conservative. He thinks we'll triple it."

"And where am I in all this, Frankie? Tell me again and again."

"In my life, if you feel sure you can face up to it. I can still afford to support you in less than the style to which you are not accustomed."

"I want it to be like that. Frankie, you may as well know it. In these terrible months I've played the stock market like mad. Anything to keep my mind off what I've done to my life. I didn't mean to lose. I wanted to win, and I did— at first."

"And?"

"There's about fifty thousand left. I want to put half of that into the Sprague Memorial. The other half—can you guess, Frank?"

"What, Claudia?"

"Maybe in trust. For kids."

He ventured no word.

Chapter 42

CONVERSATION-BALL

Myra to John Henry: "Didn't I say the first time I ever laid eyes on her that she looked like a typical madam?"

John Henry to Myra: "She was a nice woman. God only knows what must have taken place between her and Charley. God help her if he got his back up about something."

Myra to John Henry: "Yes, you certainly can't take it away from her. You could have knocked me over with a feather when I heard she walked out. I just can't get over it."

John Henry to Myra: "Dollars to doughnuts whatever happened was Charley's doing."

Myra to John Henry: "Who knows? Remember, we know less than nothing about her."

Between them the conversation-ball continued back and forth across the dinner table, and on until they lay side by side on their strange marital bed.

"I wonder if we will ever know the facts of the whole miserable business."

"What'll you bet it's his fault."

"Sure! Protect the little woman from the big bad man."

"You're not a big bad man, John Henry, by a long shot. How much do you think Brock knows? Ever since it happened, he seems to be pulling himself together, as if to make up for whatever occurred."

"I'll say. He's in the office now every day, poring over the memorial drawings with his dad. Now Charley plans to send him to Liverpool before he closes the loading-crane deal over there."

"I thought Charley was finished with promotion."

"He was, until this plum fell into his lap."

"By the way, are we going in on this big new deal?"

"You just know we are! I'm waiting to see how big a slice Charley is going to let us have. He sees money ahead in the crane, and when he sees money ahead, it's there."

"I wouldn't be surprised if Ed didn't finally want in on one of Charley's deals, now that Virgie has 'closened' up the family. How do you like my word, *closened*? I made it up. Virgie closened us."

"Ed in on it? Not a chance. That fellow from a kid up never did give a hoot about being out in front. If he wanted to whittle while we played football he whittled and let Charley be the big shot. Ed's a born whittler."

"You know, there is something to be said for whittling. I always have the feeling that Ed is laughing deep down inside himself, as he watches the rat race go by."

"What I don't understand about Ed would fill a book."

"I wonder if Clara's invitation for family dinner holds, now that the bombshell of Charley and Virgie has exploded."

"Guess she'll have to see it through. Far as I can make out, life is certainly business-as-usual with Charley."

"It's our turn next for family dinner. I wonder, now that Virgie has managed to get us together, will it stick?"

Chapter 43

TWO MEN
BENEATH ONE ROOF

IN THE LOADED HUSH FOLLOWING VIRGIE'S DEPARTURE, two men with a fresh background of sound, fury, and alleged betrayal went on with their lives beneath one roof, something resembling a new compatibility taking astonishing shape between them.

It would have been immeasurably easier for Brock to have revealed to his father the facts, even when he realized that, following the inferno of that bedroom scene and the spill of vocal garbage, there was no going back for any of them. It seemed little short of a miracle that under these harassments, the hell-fires of his personal fears should have smoldered and all but blacked out.

And now to England, on the large impending matter of the new enterprise in which his father was suddenly interesting himself. Strange bird, this man, his father. Business as usual, as if nothing untoward had happened. Anything, Brock suspected, to divert himself from the calamitous banishment of the woman out of nowhere back into the nowhere from whence he had brought her.

Yet how account for the fact that he was escaping the wrath his father might be expected to unloose upon him, for what appeared to be the terrible act of betrayal of son against father? What was going on within his old man?

This: the woman, goddamn it, whom he had taken from obscurity, asking no questions, heeding no signposts, looking the other way, had committed the mortal sin of coveting the son of the father. Decoyed him.

What chance did this boy, who was human and male, have against a whore? The word lay bitter against Charley's tongue and he spat it out. But it returned there again and again. It was as if he could not do enough in retribution.

Thus it was that the two men, their reasons diverse, went on with their lives beneath the same roof.

Chapter 44

SOMETHING ABOUT HER

FOR MONTHS CLARABELLE HAD BEEN SEEING CARL SCHLACH-ter two evenings a week. One for the Current Events Club at the church, one for motion pictures. Did that constitute going steady?

There was no other girl involved, because Carl's remaining weekdays were accounted for by night school, where he was attending courses in Business Management and Psychology of Salesmanship.

She was surprised that after her emotional embroilment with Reverend Polkinhorne she could find Carl attractive.

But this time she was not going to be singed, much less burned. No sooner had her susceptibility to Carl's person and personality begun to assert itself, than on went her protective armor.

Nevertheless, Carl Schlachter grew on one. From a sand-colored, narrow fellow in owlish eyeglasses, with no gift for extending his personality, he was emerging from her first impressions as something more than the restrained young man who appeared to say little because he had little to say.

It transpired that, while in the service, Carl had known far-flung places, looked into the fiery mouth of active Pacific battle, and visited the Asiatic continent by the grim way of invasion.

Knowledgeable in such areas as tariff, United Nations, labor unions, he entertained opinions divergent from her father's on President Eisenhower, national defense, Red China.

In some respects he reminded her of her brother, and her admiration for Anchutz was equaled only by her affection. Once or twice she caught herself up sharply in the mental act of visualizing them as brothers-in-law of fine compatibility, and immediately cast the thought from her. Never again.

All in all, the matter of Carl Schlachter and his growing encroachment into her interest was one of less tension and more inner preparedness to meet come what might with either joy or fortitude. She was braced for either.

Her mother too, whatever might have been her state of hope-rising-eternal, was outwardly accepting Carl as a matter of course.

The day before the family dinner, which had been planned and dated before Virgie's departure, Clara's old-fashioned kitchen, innocent of Deepfreeze, dishwasher, or other electric devices, was in full operation. Three freshly baked cakes, still warm from the oven, cooled on an ironing board improvised as an extra table, Clarabelle engaged in icing the last of them.

Anchutz, home at noon on Saturdays, a chair his ladder,

was stretching for a top cupboard shelf, unloading stacks of plates, cups, and saucers of Clara's best primrose-design dinner set, stamped "Made in U.S.A.," but excellent copies of willowware. In the dining room, one of Clara's kitchen aprons about his expanding middle, Ed was peeling almonds, which presently Clara would butter, salt, and brown. Two quart bottles of domestic champagne lay on a refrigerator shelf, which was already crowded with fresh uncooked vegetables, and fancy fruits that Clarabelle would stack on a Sheffield silver tray for the table centerpiece.

Even though it was to be her largest and perhaps most important function over the years, Clara's usual and methodic kitchen procedures prevailed, pots and pans washed and shelved immediately after using. Despite the manifold activities around it, her sink sparkled, her utensils shone. Mistress of her domain, she had eyes for all fronts.

"Ed, hurry with the almonds and don't leave any shell clutter. Anchutz, take down eight of everything and bring the gravy boat. Clarabelle, are you sure you don't want to ask Carl for tomorrow too?"

"I'm sure, Mama. It would look strange, as if we—we wanted it to appear he was also one of the family."

"Why not?"

"Mama, please. Anyway, he telephoned me at the office this morning and dated me for tonight."

"You are certainly getting close-mouthed, not mentioning it until now."

"In all this excitement there hasn't been time."

"Won't this be the third date with him this week?"

"Yes."

"Well, I must say, I must say."

"Mama, if I repeat the least thing, you magnify it so! We're just going to Fum Loo's for dinner—Carl likes Chinese food—and then to the Wentworth, to see *Peacock Street* in color. It doesn't mean a thing."

"But isn't it a fact you can judge a person by his tastes? Nowadays all most young men want is baseball, Westerns, and whodunits."

"Not Carl. Now he wants me to join his Thursday-night Current Events Club at the church."

"That's a grand idea. Current Events is something everyone should know about, especially with all that's going on around the world. Cold wars, hot wars—no wonder we all blow hot, blow cold."

"Carl follows things very closely. He knows all there is to know about the NAA. Do you know what that is, Mama?"

"It sounds familiar, but I don't believe I do."

"It's the North Atlantic Alliance."

"I see."

"Carl thinks we should not recognize Red China."

"There's a levelheaded young fellow if there ever was one, earning as much at twenty-eight as many a one does at thirty-eight. After all, his mother, who owns a house on the same street your Uncle Charley lives on, can't be so badly off, even if she does take roomers."

"What difference do his financial affairs make to us?"

"Nothing, but you needn't act as if I'd said something bad."

"I'm sorry, Mama," said Clarabelle, holding her sticky knife away from contact with her mother as she leaned to kiss the back of her neck. "I didn't mean it that way. But Carl's mother's finances are none of our business. Besides, how do we even know the mortgage was clear when Mr. Schlachter died?"

"Well, maybe it's none of my business, but I can have opinions, can't I? And don't forget, Carl is an only child. What a shame Virgie isn't around, to see that the two she threw together—have become such nice friends. If only we knew the facts about that woman!"

"I guess we never will, if Uncle Charley can help it."

"For the life of me, I cannot imagine what could have happened."

"Whatever happened must have come from him."

"It must have."

"It's just a shame she won't be here tomorrow. Or Claudia. What does one do on a second honeymoon with the same man? It's old dish. They've already had it."

"Mama!"

"I didn't mean it the way it sounds. But to get back to Virgie. With all her gilt hair, and those wrappers she wore—and everything—there was something about her——"

"Something about her. . . ."

Chapter 45

NO TIME FOR YOUTH

BEING ALONE HAD COME TO BE BLOSSOM'S DREAD.

The sole place where she could even momentarily overcome her depression over her second pregnancy was in Phillip's arms. Her response to his physical nearness rode down some of the anger she felt at her plight.

The second time in a little over a year! How dared he not have protected her against that! What would be left of their youth together? Her twins were lovely, to be sure, although she would have preferred to wait even for them, and Phillip had known it—but now again!

Months ahead of the morning sickness, discomfort, bulk, that ugly thickening of the face, the apprehensions, and all the while life waiting to be enjoyed and youth whizzing past like an express train.

The first winter of her marriage had been like that, and now, once more, no time for youth, for the gay things young people do. She wanted them while she and Phillip were still of an age to go about with their kind in West Grove. Reverend Donald Parker Stowe, of First Presbyterian, and Phillip were about of an age, and his wife exactly Blossom's. They were waiting, before starting their family. They went about, like the other young-marrieds, attending the country-club dances, even "night-clubbed" occasionally in St. Louis. Their parishioners loved it.

It was one thing to be young with your children, but what about being young with yourselves? Five years from now there would still be time for her and Phillip to be young with their children!

When Blossom was alone with these thoughts she ground her palms against her eyes to shut out the repetitious picture of what her second winter of pregnancy promised, or rather threatened.

Her mother was certain to be righteously joyous when she heard. Her father, so cruelly aged since his financial reverses, would react with further shock at her opposition to God's will. Since the reversal in his fortunes, the Scriptures were so frequently on his lips.

But surely God in His wisdom would understand that all she asked was a little more time in which to enjoy the temporal gift of youth.

Blossom herself, these days, was turning more and more frequently to God, emulating Phillip by interrupting her routine to fall into the attitude of prayer, exposing her forbidden thoughts, beseeching His understanding of her plight! Not now, dear God. I am afraid, so soon. Cause it not to be so. Have mercy in Your compassion. Thy will be done—but just a little more time, dear God.

Once when she was about to enter her husband's study

she drew up shortly. On his knees before his small improvised altar, Phillip was bent almost double as if by the intensity of his humility. She tiptoed out again, wondering
about the content of his prayer.

It was this: Help my child of a wife to allay her fears;
help her to better comprehend the blessing You would be-
stow upon us. Help her, my Redeemer, to understand the
incomparable gift of the life You would give to us. Grant
that our new child come, as did the twins, strong of body,
and Thy light in their eyes. Help me, O Lord, to help her
bow with humility and thanksgiving to Thy supreme and
loving will.

But daily, when the Reverend left his study and hurried
home from the rectory to look in upon her, Blossom was
too often lying face downward on her bed, too often crying.
"Stay with me, Phillip," she would implore. "This time I'm
afraid. I don't want to die and leave you and our babies."

But in her heart Blossom knew that was not her fear. She
wanted to be free of the seedling she was bearing. . . .

Chapter 46

IF ONLY I CAN KEEP
FEELING THIS WAY

THE DECISION DID NOT COME SUDDENLY. IT HAD BEEN
crouching behind Blossom's thinking for many a day. But
suddenly it had sprung. Back there in the hinterland of her
mind she must have reasoned, The longer I wait, the more
difficult. The time has come. . . .

Even in the community where she had lived her lifetime,
there was no one to whom she dared turn. She was the pastor's wife, and already the target of certain parishioners who
were critical of what they considered her too-limited participation in church activities. Too well she knew, although he
had not yet protested, that this would ultimately place Phillip
under fire.

Whatever came to pass must appear to be act of God; and
God would forgive her, because she intended, in good time,
to give Phillip the sizable family he desired.

She recalled a locally prominent physician, Dr. Shirer, who

had been suspected of malpractice. The domestic scandal of a St. Louis society woman had led to the investigation.

The doctor had not been indicted but, according to hearsay, had moved somewhat precipitously from West Grove to East St. Louis.

One day Blossom stopped in at the West Grove Public Library. From the shelf of telephone books of neighboring cities she took down the East St. Louis directory. She had no clue to the doctor's first name. So far as she recalled, she had never known it, but there was a Dr. Theobald Shirer listed at 36 Oak Hill Place.

For two weeks she made no further move. Then one day, after folding about eighty-five dollars of her household savings into her handbag and depositing her twins in the care of her mother, she set out, allegedly for a day's shopping in St. Louis.

Reverend Polkinhorne, seeing her off in their little sedan, felt relieved. She seemed more herself. He thanked God for his belief in the power of prayer and returned to the long duties of his rectory, lighter of heart than in many a day.

Oak Hill Place proved to be surprisingly pretentious, roomy mansions of another day long since outmoded, evoking nostalgic memories of more spacious and perhaps more gracious living.

Perched on a steep terrace high over the sidewalk, Dr. Shirer's residence was a far cry from the modest side-street dwelling in West Grove that Blossom believed she recalled.

This gravely handsome house quickened her nervousness, and before she could find the courage to press the bell of a side door labeled "Office" she retreated to a corner drug store to fortify herself with coffee.

She had only dim visual memory of the doctor. But after the receptionist wrote down her assumed name, "Mrs. Rollman," recommended by whom?—again a fictitious name—and she was admitted to the office, it seemed to her for the moment that she did recall him.

He was a small graying man, his desk in careful order, his face, with its clipped mustache and unremarkable features, in careful order.

"Dr. Shirer, I am here because a friend of mine who used to live in West Grove, but has since moved to California, told me about you. A Mrs. Griswold."

"Mrs. Griswold? West Grove?"

"I don't live there any more."

"But I have never set foot in the place, Mrs. Rollman," he said, referring to her card. "There must be some mistake."

New panic chased the panic already at work in her.

Not the Dr. Shirer of West Grove? Could it be that he was in hiding from his past?

"I was born in this house," he continued, "and have never practiced outside this town."

Her fright mounted and her caution receded. "But even though you are not that Dr. Shirer, you are a medical man. Help me, Doctor!"

"That is what I am here for."

"Oh, thank you, thank you. No one ever needed you more."

He regarded her with growing intentness that seemed to say, I think I suspect why; and she in turn took her cue from his manner.

"Yes, I am going to have a baby, Doctor, and I don't want to have it. Not now, I mean. I mustn't have a baby."

271

"Why?"

"Because I'm afraid, deathly afraid."

"Where is the man?"

"No, no! I am married, Doctor. Have a wonderful husband and a pair of beautiful twins. Nothing like that."

"Is this husband the father of your expected child?"

"Doctor, you don't understand. It's not like that; it's just that I don't want another so soon after the first two. I'm not ready to have one now. I mustn't."

"But why?"

"Because I want time to live, first. I see so many young wives tied down with a whole flock of babies before they've had time even to get acquainted with their husbands. I see how it is with my own marriage. No time for anything except having babies."

"Isn't that sufficient reason for living?"

"Yes—but so soon again! I adore my children, make no mistake about that."

"And your husband?"

"Yes, and my husband; he's a good man, but he shouldn't want our babies to come so fast. This one will mean three in less than two years. I want us to be young, because we are young. Besides, he's not as big an earner now as he may be later. We can still be young with our children and do more for them if we start a large family five years from now."

"Then what is it you want me to do, Mrs. Rollman, which is not your name?"

She flushed.

"Give me a way not to have it. Help me make it appear just one of those—natural—mis—mishaps."

"I see."

"Oh, thank you, Doctor, for understanding. Thank you." She leaned forward to touch his coat sleeve, which he withdrew.

"I understand that God has chosen you for the sacred responsibility of bringing a child alive. This life belongs to God and to your husband as much as to you. What right have you to destroy a life that does not belong to you alone?"

"It is done all the time, everywhere. There is even birth control."

"Yes, but this is after conception."

"It is not yet a life."

"The instant of conception is the beginning of a life. For no reason except the one you relate, you are asking me to commit murder."

"I don't look at it that way. I don't think of it that way."

"I do. And I think God and your husband would."

"He—my husband needn't——"

"Know? That leaves only God and me. And on that secret crime you plan to build your future with your husband?"

"You refuse?"

"You poor, misguided child, of course I do."

"Don't say that, Doctor."

"What is your name? Your first name?"

"I am afraid to—say."

"Don't be afraid."

"Blossom."

He leaned forward and brushed her hand lightly. "Blossom, go home now, filled with gratitude for the blessing of your pregnancy. Remember, you are touched with splendor, pretty one, foolish one."

He straightened her hat and swung her to her feet by both hands and smiled her out.

Outside it was bright blue, everything clear and so close that trees, buildings, clouds, seemed within touch.

Her car, as she headed toward the St. Louis shopping district, exceeded the speed limit.

If only I can keep feeling this way. Touched with splendor . . .

Chapter 47

ECHO

THE TABLE LOOKED BEAUTIFUL. THE FOUR ED SPRAGUES
stood off to admire it.

The seldom-used dinnerware was laid and ready, Clara's
mammoth Sheffield silver tray of in-and-out-of-season fruits
dominating it. Sprays of maidenhair fern interlaced with
small clusters of hothouse grapes were strewn from one end
of Clara's prized lace tablecloth to the other.

One tragedy, by no means minor to her, clouded the occasion for Clara. The champagne glasses were not of one
design. Four short-stemmed and four long-stemmed were all
that could be mustered from Clara's shelves and from willing
neighbors.

"Some layout," commented Ed, still shirt-sleeved, his dark
jacket hanging across the back of his chair at the head of
the table. "You girls have done yourselves proud."

"A lot of credit I get for the dirty work that doesn't show,"
growled Anchutz. "Who fixed the wobble in the table, who

275

lugged home the extra ice cubes, who beat the whites of the eggs until he was green in the face?"

His mother, a cover-up apron over her taffeta, gave a massaging stroke to the back of her son's neck. "I declare, Anchutz, that neck of yours hasn't looked clean to me since the day you were born."

"Too bad," ruminated Clarabelle critically, "we're not using the extra leaf in the table. It looks much better with it in."

"Well, why don't we ask Carl Schlachter and his mother?" quickly countered Clara. "The table does look a little bobtailed. What's the matter with calling them now? Tell them we find we have enough for two more."

"Why—at this late date, Mama—we'll have to unset the whole table."

"So what!" said Anchutz, snapping his fingers. "If you and Mom unset in a jiffy, I'll have the leaf inserted in another jiffy."

"How do we know they can come?"

"Telephone them, Clarabelle."

"You do it, Mom."

As if to a starter's pistol shot, Clara hurried to the hall telephone, returning within minutes.

"Clarabelle, remove the fruit centerpiece. Ed, stack the plates. Anchutz, climb to the top shelf for two more of everything, and don't fall."

"I *would* be the fall guy," said Anchutz, dragging his feet with a certain alacrity.

The dinner moved with Sunday slow motion. The brothers, who that forenoon had met in their capacity as ushers, now stood about the living room while drinks and appetizers were being passed, discussing church matters; Reverend Polkinhorne's idea for taxing members for a basement gymnasium; a committee report of the cost of a set of chimes; and voicing sentiments regarding bingo as a legitimate means of raising funds.

In the midst of it Myra, in the blue lace she wore at afternoon recitals, seated herself, unurged, at the venerable upright piano and spun a composition, by a Missouri composer, of rapid arpeggios, "Storm over Lake Como," into the competitive sounds of dishing-up processes from the kitchen. There, ubiquitous Mrs. Sims, whose by-the-hour waitress services had been in demand by entertaining housewives of West Grove over the years, was tying into her white apron.

On a hall settee Clarabelle, banished by her mother from the kitchen scene, was softly entertaining Carl, his mother meanwhile seated beside the piano in dutiful attitude of listening.

The meal was simple, well cooked, the turkey removed from the oven at the very second of its fullest succulence. Clarabelle's hot rolls were passed three times with no refusals, and her sweet potatoes en casserole, with banana topping, a close second.

But from the start it was apparent that the occasion was not going to lift to the ebullient level that Virgie's had achieved.

The men seemed to lend themselves to it more successfully than the women. Ed, stimulated by his unaccustomed swig of sherry and two glasses of champagne, was unobtrusive, as usual, but kept up a running patter relating to church affairs, so repetitive that his brothers spoke to one another above it, and Clara, listening with her third ear, cast anxious glances.

She laughed deep down inside herself, a little pleased. Ed was a bit drunk. He had never, bless his heart, had a let-go. Let him have it now. Relaxed, loquacious, even comical, he was all outside himself, where he had never been before.

The mixture of the scotch and the champagne was also doing its work with Brock, whose inflamed gaiety was taking the form of passing around the table and kissing the backs of ladies' necks. Clara, who was still laughing inside, wanted to cry out, "You tickle!" But she managed to contain the impulse and slap his hand away.

It was apparent to Clarabelle that neither Carl nor his mother was aware that the occasion was outside the usual. As a matter of fact, Clarabelle, who had not partaken, was nevertheless a bit heady herself. Underneath the table she and Carl were touching knees, and she dared to press back.

She regarded her father and Brock, guzzling. What did they know, while the women chattered among themselves, and her Uncle Charley declaimed loudly on his impending plan to send Brock to Liverpool to put fire under those slow-motion Britishers, of intoxication!

One indignation smoldering beneath the occasion was directed toward Charley. How dared he! Not a word of explanation from him concerning Virgie. Family had a right to know. What had happened between them? What was he, monster or mouse? Myra could scarcely keep fascinated eyes from staring in his direction. Clara averted hers, for fear of encountering in Charley's face something hidden and terrible. And what had taken place between Brock and his father, apparently uniting them? What did Brock know that they did not know?

The telephone rang and Mrs. Sims started toward the hall, Charley rising to intervene. "That must be transatlantic for me. I gave orders to transfer a call I expect from Liverpool to this number.

"You may be in flight to England this time tomorrow, Brock," he remarked to his flushed-up son as he hurried out.

In the small silence that followed, Brock rose with a noticeable sway. "To the tight little island," he said, raising his glass.

The company glanced about among themselves uncertainly and raised their tumblers.

"To Shangri-La," continued Brock, "wherever that is. To Shangri-La—la—la—"

This time the family sat immobile, exchanging fixed smiles.

"To—to the family," reiterated the mounting voice. "To the family, goddamn it, God bless it!"

"Brock!"

"To the family, I hate it, I love it. I can't live with it. I can't live without it. It's a trap. It's a kiss of death. The family! It's fearful. It's wonderful."

Ed rose to his feet.

"To the family," he repeated uncertainly, imitating his nephew in manner and voice. "To Shangri—to the la-la-la-la-la! It's a kiss! It's a trap——"

"Ed—sit down!" cried Clara, jerking him to his chair with a thump.

Glancing hurriedly over his shoulder toward the hall, Brock leaped to his chair, thrusting his glass upward at arm's length. "To Virgie," he croaked in a constricted whisper. "To Virgie, by God, and in spite of the devil!"

The family rose, glasses up, voices down.

"To Virgie!" they whispered in chorus. The name lingered an instant, then receded like an echo. . . .

Chapter 48

THE LAMP

VIRGIE FELT NO TURMOIL. SHE WONDERED ABOUT IT BUT was grateful that she was fitting back so quietly.

Gram had managed a swap, moving the occupants of her erstwhile apartment to another floor. Back in her old rooms, the period since Virgie had vacated them became wrapped in the haze of an overcrowded dream, a zany experience outside reality.

She could prove the reality of being back. There was the patch of new wallpaper where a leak had taken place two Christmases ago and Gram had pasted it over. The bedroom window that had to be propped open with a stick. The disinfectant smells of an old structure holding back its crawl of enemy invaders.

To contribute further to the tangibility of reality, she was able to buy back, at Tachman's Secondhand Emporium on Pine Street, most of the furniture she had disposed of at the time of her move.

She would have preferred all of it precisely as it had been, even to the table made of a wine keg which Ed Stutz had given her when he closed his bar. But Tachman had replaced the top with the initials carved into it, with one of smooth new plastic and it had been one of the few pieces to sell promptly and profitably.

But most of the remainder of her household, slow to move, was still piled to the rear of the overcrowded shop. Tachman, whom Virgie had known over the years, asked no questions, but sold what remained back to her at no profit, only the cost of restoration.

Even the lamp with the brass feet and globular china shade decorated with pink roses was once more on its table beside the window—the whole darling shebang, as she thought of it, as if she had never been away.

The lamp did its old-time yeoman duty. One by one, in no time at all, old friends seeing its beacon light, or hearing of the return somewhere along the grapevine, found their way up the outside staircase.

There had been deaths, unexplained disappearances, tragedies, one suicide, some rehabilitation, a great deal of inquiry for her during her absence; and a home-coming gift—box of canned goods from the downstairs grocer, and a request for her return to the five-mornings-a-week employment in the store.

Virgie could have cried at the paradoxical happiness of a returning native, and the pain with which she lived.

Poor Charley. She had not a feeling in the world against him. But this much she had known from the first crash of the terrible thunder of what had happened: there could be no way back. Did she want it? Sometimes she wondered.

Return to this environment which fitted her like the
proverbial old shoe would have been further simplified had
she been able immediately to rid herself of these paradoxical
inner conflicts. The fact that she still harbored for Charley
the residuum of something that had been affection, and
more, kept at her. She slept with it and awakened with it.
And yet she was glad to be back. She was what she was!

It was warming to see the old crowd drifting in. Familiar
faces and pastimes, the old need to stint for the small hand-
out here, the loan there, that might or might not be repaid.

She felt ashamed of the pleasure she experienced in this
drift back to driftwood. In spite of herself, it was good. But
there were gaps, and this troubled her.

Where, first of all, was Alan Bevin? Gram reported
neither sight nor sound of him. Was it possible that his
brother-in-law, the Admiral, following year-after-year attempts at his rehabilitation, had finally succeeded? Could
it be that Bevin, one-time district attorney, had perma-
nently found his way back and up? Twice over the years,
under the patient tutelage of his brother-in-law, he had
struggled back to at least temporary manhood. Where was
Bevin, gentleman-derelict, who over his long and sodden
periods had so often stumbled his way up her staircase?

Where was Peg Leg, who before the amputation had
navigated the *Linda*, queen of the barges between St. Louis
and Memphis, who needed her when sober and demanded
her when drunk? No one had seen hide nor hair of him.

Had Barney, the one-time "bouncer" at Heyman's Bar,
seen ye olde light in ye olde window since her return or had
he finally been accepted at the Denver Tubercular Hospital?

But for most part the old trek up the outside staircase was on. Virgie was back.

What was the saying about making a silk purse out of a sow's ear? Couldn't be done.

Back once more on the wall, hung from the same nail, was her only photograph of Grant, taken his first year in the Navy. A brawny, tawny fellow with her own hair and eyes. It was good to hide it no longer beneath lingerie in her dresser drawer, where it had lain during the months past.

Someday, if Grant and his Australian wife returned, she wanted it on the wall to greet him and his babies, if he had any. But, dear heaven, how unaware of the passing of time could one be! Doubtless those babies would be growing youngsters by now.

Thank God for being—home. Thank God for the discard of the living lie that the entire arrangement had been. Thank God for the old friends, and the new to come, who were already bringing their tears and cheer to her.

Even when she wept of pain, the conviction persisted that it was better this way.

And the lamp with the globular shade with pink roses showed its light through the window, and one evening up the outside staircase came the clump of footsteps quickly identifiable in her memory. They sounded like Bevins', except that they were strangely uneven, one foot coming down heavier than the other.

It was. The ruin of the man he once had been, before deteriorating into the ragtag alcoholic who had lurched into her experience. Time and again she had cleaned him up, sobered him up, kept him the night on the divan in her front room, filled him with warm breakfast, and sent him on his somewhat resuscitated way, once more the gentleman fighting his losing fight.

But the bearded one-time district attorney who now banged open the door and almost toppled as he entered was a Bevin deteriorated to such an extent that the sight of him was almost as shocking as if a man-sized ape had entered.

Tears streamed down his face into the tangle of beard, and he held out what were still finely formed hands, but blackened and furiously overgrown with hair.

"You're back," he grated drunkenly. "Why did you leave? They wouldn't tell me where you were. No—no, I'm not too drunk to know you're back. Nobody to come to all these months. I tried, without you, so help me, Virgie, but no use. I've walked along the levee night after night, wanting to slip myself in without a splash, but too big a coward to do it. A few weeks ago they gave me ten days for vagrancy. I asked the judge to make it thirty so as to get myself cleaned up and fed up and sobered up, in case you came. Something was telling me you would be back. But night after night I passed, and no light—no light— Help—me——"

She slid him into a chair, his legs straight out into the center of the room, his matted head thrown back, mouth open, fumes foul. She washed his face. "Alan, Alan, when have you washed last? Where have you been sleeping? In doorways?"

"My foot, it's on fire, and now the fire has gone up my leg. My foot—no, no, the left."

She dragged off the shoe and bloodstained sock. It stuck, and he screamed and broke out into a sweat, and she turned squeamish.

"God have mercy, I can't stand the pain!"

"Alan, that's a nail in your foot, all the way up, through—your instep. How long have you been walking on it!"

"Maybe days—maybe weeks—I can't remember how long it's been—on fire. Green fire. It's green!"

"I'll call a doctor."

"No! I'll run out of the house. Doctors can't help. I'm past that—I'm enough myself to know that. Stay with me—for God's sake."

"I will, Alan."

"Virgie, could you pull it out, to ease it up—could you, please? I know it's terrible to ask, but would you—could you——"

"The doctor——"

"Later—but just for now—could you, would you——"

"Can—you—stand—it—Alan?"

Before he could reply, she gave a jerk. With a yell he stiffened into a rigid hypotenuse, and more of his sweat sprang out.

Holding on to her own consciousness, she regarded the two-inch nail encrusted with suppurating gangrenous green, and raced for a basin of water, boiling it, tearing a clean sheet, rushing back to the filthy wound.

Kneeling, she washed and bound it, her face averted from the sour smells.

"Good, good, oh God, so good—now the other foot——" he said drowsily.

He slept as she continued at the washing of the feet.